Alison Roberts is a New Zealander, currently lucky enough to be living in the South of France. She is also lucky enough to write for the Mills & Boon Medical Romance line. A primary school teacher in a former life, she is now a qualified paramedic. She loves to travel and dance, drink champagne, and spend time with her daughter and her friends.

A SURGEON WITH A SECRET

ALISON ROBERTS

MILLS & BOON

First published in Great Britain 2021
by Mills & Boon, an imprint of HarperCollins*Publishers* Ltd,
1 London Bridge Street, London, SE1 9GF

www.harpercollins.co.uk

HarperCollins*Publishers*
1st Floor, Watermarque Building,
Ringsend Road, Dublin 4, Ireland

Large Print edition 2021

A Surgeon with a Secret © 2021 Alison Roberts

ISBN: 978-0-263-28788-2

07/21

MIX
Paper from
responsible sources
FSC C007454

This book is produced from independently certified FSC™ paper to ensure responsible forest management. For more information visit www.harpercollins.co.uk/green.

Printed and bound in Great Britain
by CPI Group (UK) Ltd, Croydon, CR0 4YY

CHAPTER ONE

'*NO...*' LACHLAN MCKENDRY put his hand over his eyes as he lowered his head. 'You can't do that...'

'I'm afraid that's what it's come to, lad. I really don't think I can take any more.'

'But you've been part of the household for as long as I can remember.' Lachlan was using his middle finger and thumb to massage his temples now. 'It will fall apart if you leave.'

'It's already fallen apart. Your mother has just fired her nurse. Again. That's three so far this year. And it's not as if she actually fires them. They walk out because she's so appallingly unpleasant to them. Impossible. She told this last one that she was an imbecile. Too stupid to live. That it was no wonder she had to work as a private nurse because nobody was ever going to marry someone who had a face like a camel. The poor girl was in floods of tears when she left this morning.'

'I can imagine. But, Mrs Tillman… *Please*… We can't lose you as well.'

Lachlan was aware of a rising anxiety. If his family's loyal housekeeper walked out, he didn't have the excuse of living and working in New York any longer. He was in London now, by comparison a mere stone's throw from the Cotswolds and the huge, old manor house he'd grown up in. His father had died many years ago and he had no siblings to share the burden of his mother so this was his responsibility. His alone, and sadly, not one he relished, that was for sure.

Josephine McKendry was not only a prickly and difficult woman, she had health issues that were serious enough to need full-time care. She would be better off in a rest home that catered for people that could afford the best but his mother was fond of saying that there was only one way she was ever going to leave that house and that was feet first, in her coffin.

'She's told me I have to administer her insulin injections.' Mrs Tillman's voice was rising as fast as Lachlan's anxiety. 'Me... I can't even stick that temperature thing into the Christmas turkey without feeling rather faint myself.'

'Mother's perfectly capable of administering her own insulin.' Unless she was having an asthma attack, of course. Or a bit of angina...

'That's as it may be.' Mrs Tillman sniffed. 'But, as you well know, she's not about to do anything she doesn't *want* to do. And she thrives on the attention. She's just got bored with the last nurse, that's all. She was just too easy to intimidate, I think, but I'm not about to let her start on *me* and that's *that*.'

'That's absolutely fair enough...' Lachlan looked up as his secretary poked her head around the door of his consulting room. He shook his head and held up his hand, indicating that he needed a few minutes before his next patient was ushered in. 'Listen... I'm going to call London Locums right now and see how soon they can provide a nurse for Mother. And I'll drive up this evening, as soon as I've finished my clinic. I'll get this sorted, I promise. But please, please don't leave, Tilly.' Using the housekeeper's old nickname was part of turning on the charm. It had always worked when he had been a kid, home from boarding school for the holidays and wanting a biscuit or some other forbidden treat from the kitchen. 'And...what about Jack?'

Mrs Tillman lived in a cottage on the estate with her husband, Jack, who had always been the head gardener on the property.

'He's not getting any younger, either. His back isn't as good as it was. Maybe it's time we both retired.'

'Oh...not just yet. *Please*. And...you know what? I think it's high time we talked about a raise in your salary, don't you? Yours and Jack's. So you can set yourselves up for a really comfortable retirement?'

There was a long moment's silence that stretched until Lachlan heard a very long sigh being released.

'You always did have me wrapped around

your little finger, young man.' Mrs Tillman sniffed again. 'I'll have some dinner ready for you tonight but I'm not making any promises.'

Lachlan headed out of the room, having assured Mrs Tillman that she was an absolute angel. He then found a smile for his secretary and receptionist who was right outside his door, clearly on a return mission to see if he was available yet. He leaned closer, to let her know that he was about to impart confidential information.

'I need a few more minutes, Sally,' he whispered. 'Bit of a personal emergency to sort out.'

'Oh...' Good grief...was Sally actually batting her eyelashes at him? 'No problem, Mr McKendry. It's not a patient waiting for you, though—it's someone from the PR department of your hospital.' She was smiling at him now. 'But I'm sure she'll understand if I say you've got an *emergency* to deal with.'

'Thank you so much. And could you find the number for a company called London

Locums and then put me through? It's rather urgent.'

'I'm onto it.'

Sally sped back to her desk and Lachlan ducked back into his office for the private call that came through a commendably short time later. It was somewhat childish, but he noticed he had his fingers crossed as he picked up the phone on his desk with his other hand.

Felicity Stephens was standing in the middle of chaos when her phone rang and it was tempting to ignore the call and get on with unpacking her suitcases—and airing out her attic apartment, of course, because it was distinctly musty after her absence of several months.

Answering the beep of an alarm or a call that could be vital was hardwired into her brain, however.

'Flick? I hope I'm not disturbing you.'

'Not at all, Julia. I'm just staring at my suitcases, trying to summon the energy to unpack them.'

'Oh…' She could hear laughter on the other

end of the line. 'I've called at precisely the right moment, then. Don't unpack—I've got another job for you.'

'Really? I hope I've got time to sleep off the jet lag.'

'No. It's urgent. I have, in fact, a rather famous plastic surgeon on the other line right now, desperately hoping that you're going to say yes to what is a very urgent position.'

'How urgent?' Flick pushed waves of her hair back from her face. It felt lank and lifeless—a bit like she felt herself after the incredibly long flight back from Australia.

'To start as soon as you can get to the Cotswolds. Preferably this afternoon.'

Flick's laughter had a hollow ring. 'You've got to be kidding.'

'He'll pay double your normal salary. And it only needs to be until he can find someone permanent, although, from what I've heard about his mother, she's known as a bit of a dragon so it might not be an instant fix. She needs careful handling, apparently, which is why I thought of you. You do "difficult" cases better than anyone I know.'

'Ha...not necessarily by choice.' But Flick had to admit she was slightly intrigued. Plus, she'd never had the chance to explore the Cotswolds and wasn't that supposed to be one of the most beautiful parts of Britain? 'Who's the famous surgeon?'

'His name's Lachlan McKendry. I've known of him for a few years, now. I guess I took notice of the articles about him because he's...well...kind of cute.' Flick could almost hear Julia shaking her head at such adolescent behaviour. 'Anyway, he grew up here—well, in the Cotswolds. Did his medical training in London but then went to the States for postgraduate degrees.

'He's a paediatric plastic surgeon who specialises in nerve reconstruction,' Julia continued. 'He's in demand at every international conference and he got headhunted to come back to London by The Richmond International Clinic, which is the private arm of St Bethel's Hospital in Richmond, but he's splitting his time between private and public work. It's his mother who needs the full-time care.'

'What's her medical history?'

Flick listened as Julia rapidly listed what added up to be a complex set of conditions that needed monitoring and frequent treatment. It certainly sounded like a challenge and that was almost as enticing as a completely new part of the world to explore.

'So…what can I tell him?' Julia spoke cautiously enough to advertise her hope that Flick could help her with this important client. 'He's on hold even though it sounds like he's probably got a waiting room full of patients. He's desperate.'

Flick eyed her suitcase. It still contained everything she needed for a temporary position. A bit of extra money would certainly come in handy after those expensive flights from the other side of the world and her car definitely needed a good run after being garaged for so long.

'Tell you what, Julia. I need a couple of hours to wash my hair and sort myself out and then I'll drive up and meet this dragon and *then* I'll decide. You can tell this Mr McKendry that, as long as his mother isn't unbearably obnoxious, I'll hang around until he can find someone permanent.'

'Oh…bless you, Flick. You're the best.'

'Hey… I'm not making any promises.' But Flick's smile was wry. 'Text me the address. I'll aim to get there somewhere around six-thirty p.m.'

Jennifer, from the public relations department, was in her forties and immaculately groomed, as if she was ready to stand in front of cameras at a moment's notice to inform the public of anything important that involved either St Bethel's Hospital or the Richmond International Clinic. She opened her briefcase the moment she sat down in Lachlan's office and produced a sheaf of papers.

'There are a few things I need to check before we release the exciting news that you'll be available for the specialist postgraduate training scheme they've been begging you to do in the wider Gloucester area.'

'No problem.' But Lachlan glanced at his watch. He would prefer to escape from London before peak-hour traffic made it too tedious. Then something clicked. The timing of this crisis with his mother was actually quite serendipitous. 'In fact, it could be that I may have to spend more time in the area during this—what is it, a twelve-week programme? I may even stay there at times and commute back to London when I need to.'

'Yes, it's twelve weeks. Is there a reason for you wanting to base yourself away from London?'

'My mother lives not far from Gloucester. She's...ah...not very well at the moment.'

'Oh, I'm sorry to hear that.' But Jennifer clearly had other things on her mind as well. 'You won't have to pull out of upcoming obligations in London, though, will you? You're due to start filming for that documentary next week.'

'Ah...yes. They've been following young Dexter since he had his surgery for the brain tumour a couple of years ago. And I'm going to do a masseteric nerve transfer surgery to treat his facial paralysis.'

Jennifer nodded. 'They want to film the

initial consultation with you, Mr McKendry, when you're explaining the surgery to him. And that'll be a good time to talk to them about having cameras and crew actually in the operating theatre. I'll come to that meeting as well. I've already spoken with Dexter's family and the neurosurgical team he's been under. Everyone's very excited about being part of the documentary.'

'It won't be a problem,' Lachlan assured her. 'It's in my diary already and I'll work around any current cases. If I could reduce my patient load over the duration of the postgraduate training course, though, that will offer more time to devote to the training. I can be available to operate as well as deliver lectures, which might be of even more benefit to the surgeons wanting to upskill.'

'Yes…' Jennifer was nodding enthusiastically. 'And it will be so valuable for interhospital relationships as well. I'll look at adjusting your rosters and outpatient clinics here myself, and then chase up any paperwork that might need covering to give you clinical privileges in other hospitals. Or at least the big ones in the area—Gloucester General and Cheltenham Central. I'm sure they'll be delighted to get more of your expertise.'

'I'm happy to oblige,' Lachlan told her. 'Even a small change can make a big difference in paediatrics. A registrar in an emergency department learning a new suturing or wound closure technique—for a serious dog bite, for example—might mean that a child is less scarred and won't need further surgery later on.'

Jennifer was scribbling notes. 'I'll put together a press release after I've talked to all the hospital administrators who are keen to get on board with this programme.' Her glance up at Lachlan was impressed. 'You're going to be rather busy for the next few months. I've never known any of our doctors to be in demand quite like this.'

Lachlan shrugged. 'I like being busy. And the commute will be a good thing. I'm going to enjoy giving my new car a bit of a run on the motorways.'

If he did end up basing himself out of town

to focus on finding a more permanent solution to the problem his mother was presenting, frequent trips to London would also give him a break from her and that would be a good thing for both of them. Better than good. Vital…

And…it was impossible to stop another thought flashing through the back of his head with the speed of light. Another small issue that he'd been putting off dealing with despite knowing that action was overdue. Being largely out of town for some time would present the perfect opportunity to bring an amicable end to his current liaison with Shayna, the very cute physiotherapist he'd met a few weeks ago. Or was it nearly two months? Too long, anyway, given that she was getting too attached.

Good grief, she'd even asked if she could have her own space in the chest of drawers in his bedroom, despite having had the 'F' rules clearly spelled out from the beginning. A relationship for Lachlan was about Fun and that was all. No Full time. No Future. No Family.

Lachlan glanced at his watch again, letting his breath out in what might have been a small sigh of relief that split-second interruption had provided.

'Speaking of which,' he told Jennifer, 'I need to get going, but just email me any queries. Or leave a phone message and I'll call back as soon as I can.' As if his phone wanted to back up his promise, a text alert sounded. Lachlan glanced at the screen, standing up as Jennifer got out of her seat. It was a message from Julia at London Locums and he could see the initial lines of the text.

Felicity's on her way to meet your mother. Good luck. She's the best—

Lachlan didn't open the message to read the rest. Yes, Julia had said on the phone that this nurse would only be deciding whether or not to take the position after she'd met his mother but getting her there was the biggest hurdle to get over. He'd had many, many years of learning that he could get pretty much anything he wanted with a combination of charm and unlimited funds available. He could feel his lips curling into a smile that was already anticipating success in dealing with the initial step of solving the problem of his mother.

'You know what, Jennifer? I'm confident that I've already got arrangements in place that will make this all run as smoothly as possible. I might even be back by tomorrow morning and have some time to meet up. We can thrash out the final details of the training programme. Maybe you can give me some tips for working with that film crew as well.'

Jennifer gave him an unreadable look. 'I think you'll manage just fine, Mr McKendry. You seem to have everything well under control.'

Yes…

He *did* have things under control. The issue of dealing with an aging and difficult family member was nothing he couldn't handle and Lachlan McKendry had every intention of doing so with kindness and patience.

Josephine McKendry was his mother, after all, and you only ever got one of them.

And how could you not feel happy when you could stay in the fast lane and pass everything else on the M4 as if they were barely moving? He settled a little deeper into the butter-soft leather seat of his brand-new, Dolomite Silver Porsche 911 Carrera. Zero to one hundred kilometres an hour in four point two seconds. Not that he'd tried that out yet, of course, but it would be fun...

The average time from London to Gloucester was a couple of hours but Lachlan wasn't going that far because the family estate was in a deeply forested pocket amongst Cotswold villages. He'd be able to shave at least forty minutes off that kind of journey time. The inbuilt sat nav in his dashboard was already recalculating his arrival time as Heathrow Airport flashed past. He should be at his destination by about six-thirty p.m. Just in time for an aperitif before one of Tilly's delicious dinners.

A vocal instruction was enough to raise

the volume level of the music coming from a sound system that was one of the best Lachlan had ever heard but he wanted something a bit more upbeat. Something that fitted in with his current optimism.

'Play "Living on a Prayer" by Bon Jovi' he instructed.

He could totally get on board with the chorus of that song. He was, literally, almost halfway there already.

This couldn't be right, surely…

Flick slowed her bright yellow Volkswagen Beetle as she turned past ornate, wrought-iron gates to find herself on a tree-lined driveway that was so long she couldn't even see a house. It looked like the entrance to a National Park. Or a residence of a minor Royal, perhaps? But, then, Julia had told her that Mrs McKendry wasn't a 'Mrs' at all. She was Lady Josephine because her now deceased husband had been knighted for his services to cardiothoracic surgery or something. She'd also said the family was seriously wealthy and that the house she was going to had probably had McKendrys living in it for centuries.

'You'll love it, Flick,' she'd added. *'A real taste of old-fashioned, upper-class England. Bit different from what you grew up with in Australia, I'm guessing.'*

A 'bit different' was already an understatement. Finally coming to the end of the driveway, Flick felt her jaw dropping as she took in the circular drive with a central garden and ornate fountain and the enormous house behind it. The beautiful stonework and countless lead-lighted windows, a slate roof that looked many hundreds of years old and the sense of history it evoked sent a shiver down her spine. The stories that would have seeped into those stones...

Flick had worked in many different places in the years she'd been with various medical locum agencies based in both Sydney and London. She'd worked with aeromedical retrieval services, in both private and public hospitals, general practice clinics, private homes and even on superyachts but she'd never felt like she was stepping back in time like this. She should be in a small carriage, being pulled by a couple of horses, she decided, as she parked her little yellow car nearest the door at the top of a wide sweep of steps. She should be wearing a long, boofy dress and any second now the doors would be flung open to reveal a butler ready to show her into…ooh…a drawing room, perhaps? Or a library? She stood at the bottom of the steps for a moment longer, staring up at the walls of the house as a smile stretched across her face.

She was still smiling as she turned at the sound of gravel being spat out from beneath fast-moving tyres but it faded as an expensive-looking silver car came to a stop that was abrupt enough and close enough to send small pebbles to hit her boots and it was completely gone by the time the driver emerged from the car and walked towards her.

Wow…

It wasn't a coherent word in Lachlan's head.

This was more like a sensation that had started in his eyes but was now trickling down to every cell in his body. A rather overwhelming sensation but that was entirely appropriate, given that he was actually walking towards what had to be the most gorgeous woman he'd ever seen in his life.

She had blonde hair that didn't quite touch her shoulders and it was parted in the middle. Not quite curly but wavy enough to make a delicious frame for a face that was, quite simply, perfect. Big blue eyes. A cute snub nose. A generous mouth that looked as if it was made for laughter.

The rest of her body was just as amazing. It only took the briefest of glances to take in slim legs covered in faded denim and tucked into knee-high boots, a soft white shirt that hung loose onto her hips. The denim waistcoat and a couple of unusual, silver chain necklaces told him instantly that this woman had her own style and personality. That she was…different…

It was only a fraction of time before he looked back at her face but there was no hint of a smile there. That didn't stop Lachlan from finding his own—the one that never failed.

'My day just got a whole lot better,' he told her. 'If you're the Felicity Stephens that's come from London Locums, that is.'

She was staring at him.

'If you're who I think you are, I was told that you're a doctor?'

'That's right. I'm Lachlan McKendry. It's my—'

She interrupted him. 'A plastic surgeon, yes?'

'Also correct.' That direct stare was a little disconcerting now. 'Why do you ask?'

'Well, I'm wondering if it's in a professional capacity that you're assessing my body in quite such an obvious manner.' There was a definite hint of a smile on her face now, as she turned away from him. 'I'm quite happy with my boobs as they are, thanks.'

Oh…he wanted to say that he agreed wholeheartedly but he wasn't about to open his mouth again in a hurry. He'd never had a slap like that when he'd tried to turn on the charm. Okay…flirt a little. Who wouldn't when they met the most beautiful girl in the world? And maybe that was the problem. Looking like that, this locum nurse probably had to deal with being hit on all the time. No wonder he had annoyed her and that was the last thing he wanted to do.

He needed to fix this.

And fast.

Felicity Stephens was the key to his being in control of this current disturbance in his life and Lachlan couldn't afford to antagonise her. Taking the steps two at a time, he caught up with her just before she reached for the lion's head brass door knocker. He also caught her gaze.

'I'm so sorry, Felicity,' he said quietly. 'I *was* a little overexcited to see you—but it's because I've had a rather difficult day and I suspect you might very well be the answer to my prayers.'

She held his gaze, as if gauging whether his apology was genuine or not. Lachlan could almost feel himself lowering his guard—just enough that she would see a glimpse of a version of himself that nobody ever really got to see.

She blinked. 'And I probably overreacted,' she said. 'I could blame jet lag because I only got off a flight from Australia at lunchtime today. Or…' There was a flash of humour in those astonishingly blue eyes. 'It could be being called "Felicity" that got my back up. I'm Flick, except for official identification, like in my passport.'

Flick…

A name that was as different as she was. This woman was getting more intriguing by the minute but Lachlan didn't say anything. He just nodded as he pushed open the enormous front door of his childhood home.

'Please come in,' he invited. 'I'm quite sure that my mother is going to be just as delighted to meet you as I am.'

CHAPTER TWO

'WHO ARE *YOU*?' Lady Josephine McKendry looked a lot less than delighted when she was introduced to Flick.

'This is Felicity Stephens, Mother.' Lachlan straightened from having kissed his mother's cheek. 'One of the best nurses that London Locums has on their books, I've been told. We're lucky enough that she happens to be available and she's come to meet you. Oh, and she prefers to be called "Flick".'

Lady Josephine snorted rather inelegantly. 'That's the name for a fire engine, not a person. Didn't there used to be some dreadful children's song about that?' She rested a piercing gaze on Flick for a breath before turning back to the window beside her armchair. 'You can both go away. I'm not in the mood to be shown off to someone like some interesting medical specimen.' She seemed to be completely focused on the beautiful, formal garden that was fading into the dusk as part of the much wider view offered from the first floor of this house.

Flick caught Lachlan's gaze. She should give up now and just walk out because it was quite clear she wasn't wanted. Needed, perhaps, but that wasn't her problem, was it? This was Lachlan McKendry's mother and he was here so he could look after her, even if it was more than a little inconvenient.

But something was stopping her.

Something that was complex enough to intrigue her.

The tension between this mother and son was palpable. It almost felt as if Josephine hated her child but what mother could ever do that? It also felt like her lack of warmth was something that was still hurtful to Lachlan even though he had to be a few years older than Flick, who was in her early thirties. You'd think that she would, at least, be proud of a son who had achieved so much at an early age. A son who was famous, ad-

mittedly very good looking and…sophisti-
cated? Was that the word Flick needed to
encompass the kind of charm—charisma,
even—that this man exuded?

But that was something else that was intriguing. Because Flick knew that Lachlan's
persona was a front. A shop window that
gave nothing away about what could be on
offer if you were allowed inside. She might
not have guessed, despite having cultivated
an image of her own that prevented anyone
getting close to who she really was, except
for that tiny moment in time—no more than
a heartbeat, really—when he'd apologised
for being such a blatant flirt and she'd seen
something in his eyes that had had nothing
to do with the over-confident, charming and
superficial barrier he'd created.

She'd had a similar moment of insight
when Lady Josephine had glared at her before turning away. Just enough to know that
this rather frail, older woman was fright-
ened.

Of dying? That would be understandable,
given her fragile health. She wasn't exactly

geriatric, either. If Lachlan was in his mid-thirties, Lady Josephine might only be in her early seventies. Late sixties, even?

Or was it because of something even deeper than that? Dying alone, maybe, because of what had happened to cause such a rift between herself and her son?

Whatever. In spite of the bone-deep weariness that only jet lag could create and an emptiness that made Flick realise it had been far too long since she'd eaten anything substantial, she couldn't walk out on the puzzle these people presented. People who had everything, it would seem—the most gorgeous house she'd ever seen, in the most idyllic setting, and unlimited funds to keep it that way—but they were both miserable. No, that was the wrong word. They would probably both empathically deny that they were less than happy. Because they didn't want to recognise it themselves?

She took a step closer to Lady Josephine's chair. 'I don't need to be here for long,' she said calmly. 'But you might need some assistance until you can choose your own private nurse. Could I help you with your evening medications, perhaps?'

Lady Josephine sniffed. 'You're far too pretty to be looking after old, sick people,' she said. 'Stuck in the middle of nowhere.'

'I'll take that as a compliment,' Flick murmured. She didn't dare look at Lachlan because that would remind them both of that small altercation when they'd met.

Lady Josephine turned her head. 'Why aren't you married?' she demanded.

Flick's eyes widened. 'Are *you* married?'

'That's none of your damned business.'

Flick's smile was one-sided. 'Exactly.'

One side of Lady Josephine's mouth twitched, as if she was amused by the response, but she hadn't finished.

'Who was your last patient?'

'An elderly gentleman who lived in Sydney, Australia. His name was Stanley.'

'What was wrong with him?'

'He was unwell with quite a few underlying health issues. A bit like yourself, I believe.'

'What happened to him? Why did you leave?'

'He died,' Flick said quietly.

Lady Josephine snorted again. 'You didn't look after him very well, then, did you?'

'Mother...' Lachlan's protest was ignored by both the women.

'He was quite happy with my care,' Flick told his mother. 'Mind you, it was a bit hard to tell because he covered up how he was really feeling by being impossibly grumpy and demanding. Also a bit like yourself, I suspect, Lady Josephine.'

She could hear a stifled laugh from Lachlan's direction. More surprisingly, it was obvious that Lady Josephine was on the point of losing her own battle not to smile.

'You'll do,' she said, turning back to the window again. 'You're feisty. I rather like feisty.' She waved her hand. 'Go over to that table over there and sort out the mess my housekeeper's made with all my medications. The stupid woman couldn't even bring herself to check my blood sugar level.'

'That sounds like a good place to start, then.' Again, Flick caught Lachlan's gaze as she walked past him to get to the table.

Her glance was a warning not to take anything for granted, however. 'Low blood sugar can make anyone grumpy,' she murmured. 'I might as well make myself useful while I'm here.'

Lachlan's smile was unexpectedly genuine. 'Thanks. I'll go and make *myself* useful too, and see what Tilly's organised for our dinner. It'll be worth staying for, I promise.'

Tender roast beef and vegetables like crispy potatoes and soft, sweet triangles of pumpkin, Yorkshire puddings and a rich gravy made from pan drippings had always been Lachlan's absolute favourite meal. Tilly had set the table in the formal dining room but Lachlan had instinctively vetoed the choice.

'We'll eat here in the kitchen,' he told the housekeeper. 'It's so much more homely and…and I'm rather hoping to persuade this nurse to stay. I think she might even have Mother wrapped around her little finger already.'

Tilly chuckled. 'That'll be the day. Do you want to take her tray up or shall I?'

'I'll do it. If Flick's not done with the medications, I can give her a hand. Poor thing must be dead on her feet. She only flew in from Australia today.'

'Nothing that a bit of my good home cooking won't fix, I'm sure. And a good sleep. I've got the guest suite made up for her and that's a very comfortable bed.'

Mrs Tillman was not only the head gardener's wife and the housekeeper, she was cook, cleaner, secretary and mother figure and Lachlan had no hesitation in giving her a hug.

'You're the one person in my life that I've always been able to rely on, you know that?'

'Oh, get away with you.'

Mrs Tillman gave him a push and Lachlan was laughing as he turned to find that Flick had come into the kitchen. Oh, help... had she heard what he'd just said? And did it matter if she had? Yeah, it kind of did. For whatever reason—even if it was just to persuade Flick to stay in the house—it seemed of paramount importance to impress her, and revealing that his childhood housekeeper had been more important than anyone else in his life might seem...well...unimpressive? A bit pathetic, even?

But she was smiling. 'Something smells *amazing*,' she said. 'The last meal I had was the plastic kind you get on planes and I can't even remember how long ago that was now. I'm Flick, by the way...' She held out her hand. 'And I'm guessing you're Mrs Tillman?'

Tilly wiped her hand on her apron before taking Flick's and grasping it warmly. 'I am.' She turned back to the oven to take out a steaming tray. 'I expect Her Ladyship's probably been telling you how useless I am with needles or the sight of blood.'

Lachlan knew perfectly well that Flick had heard even more disparaging comments about Tilly but there was no flicker of agreement on her face. Instead, she took another deep, appreciative sniff. 'She did say that she was ready for her dinner and I can see why she must be looking forward to it. Oh, wow...are those Yorkshire puddings? I tried to make them once and they came out like punctured tyres.'

Lachlan joined in the laughter and the kitchen suddenly seemed even more homely and welcoming than he'd remembered it being.

'Sit yourselves down,' Mrs Tillman ordered. 'I'll serve up, take a tray upstairs and then I'll be off home to my Jack. He'll be wanting his dinner, too. Lachlan, you can show Flick here where her rooms are, can't you?'

'It would be my pleasure.' Lachlan smiled at Flick. 'Tilly's made up the best suite in the house for you.'

'But...' Flick was frowning. 'I haven't decided whether I'm staying or not.'

'You can't drive back to London tonight. Not when you're jet-lagged and hungry. Besides—' he tried another smile—the one where he knew that those shutters came down for a blink of time '—I just happen to have a highly recommended bottle of Australian wine in the fridge and this seems like the perfect moment to open it.'

Flick's face stilled and she was holding their eye contact. Lachlan knew he should break it before it became far more significant than it actually was, but he couldn't. He was caught by something he could see in that blueness that was even darker in this shadowy old kitchen. Something he couldn't begin to define but it was doing something weird to him. This had nothing to do with the overwhelming attraction he'd been aware of when he'd first set eyes on this woman. No…whatever this was, it was making him feel both sad and happy at the same time. What on earth was that about?

It was a moment that felt utterly silent, which was crazy because there was a background of busy clattering of plates and pans and cutlery. A moment that also felt a lot longer than it probably was. It was Flick who shifted her gaze first.

'Go on, then,' she said. There was a smile in her voice even if it didn't quite reach her lips. 'I reckon that's the best offer I've had all day.'

Lachlan hid the smile that wanted to appear as he headed for the fridge. He hadn't made his best offer yet, by any means. Whatever it took, he was going to try and make sure that Flick would decide to stay. Preferably for as long as possible. Not just because she was the most beautiful woman in existence. Maybe it was because she seemed to know exactly how to handle his mother, which was nothing short of a small miracle. Or maybe it was because, despite it being disturbing, it felt like that strange way she'd made him feel was somehow important.

Vital, even?

'This is, quite possibly, the most delicious dinner I've ever eaten in my life.' Flick eyed the piece of fluffy Yorkshire pudding, dipped in gravy, on the end of her fork as she tried to decide whether she had room for one last mouthful. With a sigh of defeat, she popped it in her mouth, closing her eyes to savour this final morsel. She could feel the heat from the cream-coloured Aga stove at her back and the unevenness of the flagstone floor beneath her feet, she could smell the aromas of the wonderful food they were eating and still taste the smoothness of that wine that had accompanied the meal. But, most of all, she was aware of the man who was sitting at the end of this old, oak kitchen table. There was an energy about him that was disconcerting. Impossible to ignore.

She opened her eyes. 'I'm pretty sure that your mother's medication is all up to date, although I'll check again. But what kind of other assistance does she need in the evenings?'

Lachlan put down his fork and reached for his wine glass. 'She doesn't actually *need* any assistance at all,' he said. 'She's only sixty-three and she's perfectly capable of looking after herself—she just chooses not to when it comes to medication. After various crises, including diabetic ketoacidosis from not taking her insulin, a coma from taking too much and an asthma attack that could well have been fatal if Tilly hadn't found her, I decided that a full-time medical carer was essential. Actually, being in a rest home would have been more practical, given that I was living in New York at the time, but Mother absolutely refuses to leave this house.' His smile was wry.

'I sometimes wonder if it was my father she fell in love with or the family mansion that he'd inherited. He was quite a lot older than her—about eighteen years—so it can't have been too much of a surprise that he died first.'

'How long ago was that?'

'Hmm…' Lachlan drained his wineglass and reached for the bottle on the table. He reached for Flick's glass but she shook her head.

'I'd be out for the count if I had any more.' And, no matter how tired she felt, she didn't want to sleep just yet because it was more compelling to listen to what Lachlan had to say. To find out more about what it was that made this man so…so *intriguing…*

He refilled his own glass. 'I was a senior registrar,' he told her. 'So it's quite a few years ago now. I'd just signed up for a rotation in cardiothoracic surgery, which pleased my father so much he booked his favourite table at the Ritz for a family celebration. He collapsed before his entrée arrived, with a massive heart attack.'

'Oh, *no*...'

'It was quite lucky we were in the city. It meant he was in hospital getting the best treatment almost within minutes. And it looked as though he was recovering but there was too much damage to his heart muscle. He had a cardiac rupture a week or so later and died instantly.'

Flick was silent for a moment, her brain retrieving something Lachlan had said. Or maybe the tone in which it had been said.

'Was that what made you change your mind about which specialty you wanted to follow?'

'What?' Lachlan looked astonished. 'Good grief, no. It was what gave me the freedom to do what I wanted to do. Up until then my destiny had been sealed. I went off to boarding school in time for my sixth birthday and the headmaster introduced me to everyone as the boy who was going to become a famous surgeon just like his father.'

Flick's jaw dropped. 'You got sent to boarding school when you were *five*?'

Lachlan's gaze slid away from hers as if he'd revealed more than he'd intended to. He reached for his glass again.

'It wasn't so bad,' he said. 'I got to come home in the holidays. If I did well in my exams, my father was happy. If Father was happy, then so was Mother and, if they were both happy, I got to do whatever I liked.'

Flick's heart was being squeezed so hard it hurt, imagining that small boy who was being sent away from home. Who had learned to work hard at school to try and earn his parents' approval. Love, even...?

She kept her tone light, however. Instinct told her that Lachlan would not appreciate pity. 'So what was it that you liked to do?'

Lachlan shrugged. 'I helped Jack in the gardens. Persuaded Tilly to give me biscuits. I read a lot and... I guess I know every square inch of the patch of woodlands we own. It's the most beautiful place in the world. Not that I've set foot in it for years, mind you.'

'When did you head to New York?'

'As soon as I could. I changed that surgical rotation from cardiothoracic to plastics and then kept going with postgraduate study. I'd always been fascinated by plastic surgery. I know that makes most people think of something like breast augmentation but that is of no interest to me whatsoever.' He caught Flick's gaze and held it. 'I see it as a way to repair things that can enhance someone's *life*. To improve a disabling disfigurement, perhaps. Or use the magic of microsurgery to restore function even more than appearance.'

His passion was unmistakable and Flick cringed as she remembered that flippant remark she'd made.

'Sorry,' she murmured.

Lachlan shrugged again. 'Doesn't matter. I shouldn't be boring you with my opinions. Or with the family history, either.'

'Knowing more about your mother is important.' Flick couldn't call Lady Josephine his 'mum' because it just didn't feel right. 'If I'm going to take the position here.'

She saw the flash of hope in Lachlan's eyes. 'What do you want to know?'

'Is it too far-fetched for me to be thinking that her grumpiness might be due to depression?'

'I wouldn't say that she's ever been a particularly happy woman,' Lachlan said slowly. 'But her life certainly changed a lot after Father died. I put a lot of that down to her late onset Type One diabetes and the angina on top of the asthma she's always had, but I guess her social life pretty much vanished over the same time period. She loved being a prominent surgeon's wife. A "Lady". A local celebrity, really. There were always public appearances and lots of parties and dancing. Mother used to be a patron of all sorts of things as well and that's all in the past.' He was frowning now. 'You could well be right. It might explain her lack of interest in coping with her medications. And, if that's the case, it might make a real difference if it got treated.'

And there it was again. That flash of what looked like hope. This time, it didn't have anything to do with the idea that someone else might shoulder the burden of caring for the difficult person his mother had become. Rather, it was hope that there could be a way of helping Lady Josephine get more joy out of life. However dysfunctional Lachlan McKendry's relationship with his mother was, he cared about her.

The knowledge added another layer to that image of a lonely little boy being sent off to boarding school far too early and learning to earn his father's approval. Had that small child felt a mother's rejection when he'd needed his own love returned? No wonder he was hiding behind an image that would never invite pity. A charismatic, privileged playboy type of image that would normally have alienated Flick instantly. But she'd seen behind the shutters, hadn't she? Just for an instant or two but she knew there was a very different person there.

A person that was capable of touching something she'd believed had died in her a long time ago—the ability to feel an interest in a man that was genuine enough to generate physical attraction.

She could feel it now. A tingle, deep in her belly that stirred memories poignant enough to almost bring tears to her eyes. Which was ridiculous. She was just over-tired, that was what it was.

'I really need to get some sleep,' she told Lachlan.

'Of course. I'll show you your room.' Lachlan was on his feet instantly but then he paused. 'Have you…?' He shook his head. 'I don't want to put any pressure on you but…'

He wanted to know if she was going to stay and look after his mother. Of course he did. If she left in the morning, he'd have to stay and make other arrangements and he would probably need to adjust his schedule. She shouldn't stay, Flick thought. Not with that unexpected revelation her body had just provided, which was every bit as unprofessional as the way Lachlan had been trying to flirt with her when they'd met on the doorstep.

But there was a woman upstairs who was

unhappy enough not to care whether she took the medications she needed to prolong her life or at least make it more comfortable. A son who cared deeply about his mother even if he'd never been loved enough as a child. And there was this amazing house surrounded by woodland that was, apparently, the most beautiful place in the world.

Maybe it was that glass of wine on top of a good dose of jet lag but Flick felt like she'd stepped into some kind of modern fairy tale. She was in a magic setting and there was the equivalent of a wicked queen upstairs. Tilly was a loyal servant and Lachlan...well, he could easily step into the role of a prince.

What did that make her?

A good fairy?

A potential princess?

Simply too tired to think clearly? Yep, that seemed to be what it was because Flick had to catch the edge of the table as she stood up, her weariness enough to make her unsteady on her feet.

She could see concern in Lachlan's eyes

now, along with the question she hadn't answered.

'You know what?' She held his gaze. 'I *have* decided.'

She could see right into those dark eyes now. No shutters. He wanted her help. He needed it. How could she possibly refuse?

She couldn't.

'I'll stay,' she said. 'If that's what your mother wants.'

'I'm sure she will.' Lachlan was smiling. 'She said you were feisty. She likes you.' There was more than relief in his eyes now. Flick had the impression that *he* liked her as well.

The feeling was mutual, then. Not that there was any question of stepping over any professional boundaries. Something that, even this morning, would have been unthinkable on a personal level and now, with Lachlan McKendry about to employ her, was totally unacceptable on a professional level.

Flick let her breath out in a sigh of relief. Because there was no need to think about that familiar tingle and what it might mean. Every reason not to, in fact.

'Are you sure I don't need to check on your mother before I go to sleep?'

'She's got an alarm. Here…' Lachlan went to an old, pine dresser at the end of the kitchen and picked up a small electronic device, like a pager. 'You take this. She'll ring if she needs attention.'

And there she was. Employed as Lady Josephine's private nurse with absolutely no idea what was going to happen. But that was okay. Flick thrived on a challenge. Facing up to them had been what had saved her many years ago—the only thing that had made life worthwhile, even. She loved new places. Something different—and this was as different as it could get. If it wasn't a fairy tale, it was definitely a mystery and it certainly wasn't going to be boring.

CHAPTER THREE

BEING IN THE spotlight had never fazed Lachlan McKendry.

Perhaps it was because he'd grown up with parents who'd had more than their fair share of media attention. Or that he'd worked hard enough at school to attract attention for his academic achievements as much as his family connections and had then gone on to garner international acclaim for his skills. If he was really honest, however, he'd also always rather enjoyed the way it made people look at him as if he was someone special. Especially women.

Like the way he was being watched right now from more than one direction as his introductory part in Dexter Thompson's documentary was being filmed. Jennifer from PR was in the background, with a tablet device in her hands, watching his every move, and the stare from a young sound technician with a cheeky smile was unashamedly blatant. Even the documentary producer who would be interviewing Lachlan on his own very soon, to get his personal take on the case, was letting her gaze linger without bothering to hide her interest as Lachlan continued with the physical examination of how severe Dexter's facial paralysis was.

'Can you raise your eyebrows for me? That's great... Now, close your eyes and keep them closed if you can.' Lachlan used his middle finger and thumb to pull the skin above and below the eyes to provide resistance. It was very obvious that Dexter had almost no control of half his face. 'Okay... puff out your cheeks for me. And—last one—show me your teeth...'

He had questions for Dexter about the irritation he got in one eye due to the impaired eyelid movement, the mouth ulcers he experienced frequently and the difficulties he had in eating and drinking because one side of his mouth couldn't function normally. Sometimes Dexter's only responses were a nod or shake of his head because his speech wasn't always clear, but when it came to admitting that he often drooled or lost pieces of food, his hesitation and the way he dropped his gaze spoke volumes about just how much this problem was affecting his life.

When he heard what could have been a soft sound of distress from Dexter's mother, Bridget, who was sitting beside him, Lachlan was concerned that he'd upset his young patient enough for them to need to stop filming for a while, but Dexter simply turned his head to catch his mother's gaze and then took a deep breath, looking back at Lachlan and clearly ready to continue. Lachlan thought it was his mother's presence that gave Dexter renewed confidence but he changed his mind when he glanced briefly in the same direction himself.

Bridget was one woman here, at least, who wasn't remotely interested in looking at Lachlan as anyone other than the doctor who had the ability to help her son. She wasn't even looking at him at all, in fact, because her attention was firmly fixed on her son. There was an unmistakeable, quiet pride in her face but the overwhelming interpretation of that look was one of absolute love and that gave Lachlan an odd twist of emotion, not unlike the one he'd had when he'd first met Felicity Stephens—that very strange mix that was both sad and happy at exactly the same time.

The feeling was almost identical, in fact, and in that split second of awareness he decided that it was more sad than happy, which made it something to push aside as hard as necessary to make it disappear completely. There was something far more important to focus on, anyway. It was time to move on to explaining his part in Dexter's treatment.

'So this is a diagram of all the nerves in your face, Dexter.' The medical illustrations department of St Bethel's Hospital had done a great job of making this colourful, laminated poster. 'These yellow lines are the facial nerve and its branches.' He touched a point on the diagram. 'This is the main trunk and this bit here is what we call the motor nucleus.'

A cameraman had stepped forward to zoom in on the poster. Dexter was nodding, managing to look as if they hadn't already rehearsed this quickly beforehand, and Lachlan was keeping his language as simple as possible because he knew this programme would be mostly watched by people with no medical training.

'The good thing about an acoustic neuroma, which is the kind of brain tumour you had taken out a couple of years ago, is that it's benign, which means it isn't cancer. That doesn't mean we can leave it there, of course, because it keeps growing and can cause complications like the loss of balance and build-up of fluid inside the skull that you experienced.'

Maybe when he was talking to the producer, he could go into more detail about how dangerous the tumour could be because of its proximity to the brainstem and the fatal outcome that could happen.

'A bad thing about an acoustic neuroma,

though,' he continued, 'is that it grows very close to the facial nerve and the surgery to remove it can cause damage and swelling and lead to facial paralysis. Like yours. But another good thing is that you had your surgery less than two years ago, which means there's less scarring on the facial nerve and the chances are much better that the nerve transfer we're going to do will be successful.'

Dexter lifted his head, the camera changed direction from the poster to his face and Lachlan knew that the next shot would capture the hearts of any audience, as the lad instinctively returned Lachlan's smile.

At fifteen years old, Dexter should be beginning to explore the new world of relationships that teenagers found themselves in but the damage to his facial nerve gave him a disfigurement that made even smiling at a girl something to be avoided at all costs because only one side of his mouth could curl up, leaving the other side to seemingly droop further and the eye on the same side to be too wide open and staring, as it was now. Even more poignantly, the unparalysed side of Dexter's face was shining with hope.

It wasn't just the future audience of this documentary whose hearts would be captured. Right now, Lachlan was aware of the catch in his own chest—the kind that had been what had drawn him in to this branch of medicine and kept him here, fascinated by every case and determined to make a real difference in the lives of children and young people just like Dexter. It was hard not to get too emotionally involved in a case like this but, unlike that confused feeling he wasn't even going to try and analyse, Lachlan knew exactly how to handle this kind of emotion. You used every ounce of skill you had to get the best possible outcome, and when it was a success there was immense satisfaction to be found and that was a form of happiness all in itself.

This time, Bridget had to reach for some tissues. 'It's been so hard,' she said quietly. 'Kids can be so cruel, can't they? The bullying and so on...' She wiped her eyes and gave Dexter an apologetic smile. 'Sorry,' she mouthed silently.

Maybe they would cut that bit out later because that was when the filming of that segment ended. Lachlan would spend a few minutes explaining the masseter nerve transfer surgery, have a brief conversation with the producer that was likely to focus on how life-changing the procedure could be for Dexter and then he had some time to himself for the first time in two, long days. He'd been busy tying up cases he'd been involved in, to help clear his schedule to allow time for the postgraduate training course, ever since he'd come back to London the morning after Flick had agreed to take on the position as his mother's private nurse.

Dexter and his mother were getting ready to leave his consulting room and Lachlan saw Bridget pause to drop a wad of used tissues into the bin. The random thought that he was quite sure his own mother had never shed a tear on his behalf gave him another one of those strange twists of an emotion he didn't want to explore. At least it was fainter, this time, but it made him wonder what was going on in that Cotswold manor house.

He'd arranged for his mother's GP to visit yesterday to give her a thorough check-up and discuss her management with her new nurse, but what Lachlan really wanted to know was how Flick was coping with a difficult client. There was definitely anxiety there that she might pack her bags and walk out like so many others before her, despite the fact that Tilly had told him in last night's phone call that Flick was coping extraordinarily well. What was the phrase she'd used? Oh, yes…that she had Lady Josephine 'eating out of her hand'.

That would be something to see. The weird feeling came back a bit stronger then and Lachlan decided it must have something to do with concern for his mother. Guilt that he wasn't doing quite enough, perhaps? He needed to get back home and see how things were going.

No. He *wanted* to get back home, he realised. As soon as possible…

An appointment had been made for tomorrow for the electromyography tests that would map any nerve activity still functioning on the paralysed side of Dexter's face but Lachlan wouldn't have another part to play until the actual day of the surgery and there were still some boxes for Jennifer to get ticked before the film crew could be allowed into the operating theatre.

'There hasn't been a date pencilled in for the surgery yet, has there?' he asked her.

'Not yet, no. Given the arrangements that need to be made, including input from the hospital's ethical committee regarding the filming and publicity, I can't see it happening before next week. Is that a problem?'

'Not at all. I was just thinking that it could be a good time to line up the first lectures for the training programme in the next few days. What was the session that Cheltenham Central wanted to start with? Suturing techniques?'

'Yes. With specific reference to dealing with dog bites.' Jennifer shook her head. 'Seems like they must get a lot of them.'

'They can leave devastating scarring on a

young child. I have an entire lecture written on that topic that I delivered in the States. It won't take me long at all to make it more relevant with some UK statistics. Have you got suggested seminar times?'

'Yes.' Jennifer opened a new screen on her device. 'Okay…there's an open session available for tomorrow, actually, but that's far too soon. There's another one, the day after tomorrow, on Thursday. How does that sound?'

'I could do both.' Lachlan nodded in response to the producer, who had signalled that they were ready to start filming again. 'I'm planning to head back to the Cotswolds this evening,' he told Jennifer. 'I may as well stay for a few days and get things really rolling. Can I leave that with you?'

'Absolutely. I'm sure they'll be delighted to get things started and short notice shouldn't be a problem because they're planning to film any sessions there for anyone who can't make themselves available. You're okay with that?'

Lachlan nodded. He was obviously going

to have to get used to having cameras around more often.

'Do you want to make yourself available for surgeries as well?'

He nodded again.

'Mr McKendry? Are you ready?' The documentary crew was waiting for him.

'I am indeed,' he responded.

He was ready for anything. Including an incredibly busy schedule with all the extra commitments being arranged and spending a lot more time in his childhood home. He was, in fact, looking forward to being there more than he had done in…well…decades. Probably not since those first school holidays when he'd been released from boarding school and would be filled with hope that being back in his beloved woodland would instantly make his world much closer to perfect.

Lachlan had long ago given up believing in fairy tales where a magic wand could be waved or a magic place could provide an escape from reality. Hope had given way to acceptance of the way things were by the time he'd been about Dexter's age and that had been followed by a determination to create his own world. One that he could control. One that could provide all the happiness he needed.

He sat back at his desk and tipped his head back a little, closing his eyes as he felt the brush of the sound technician's fingers as she clipped on his lapel microphone again.

The sooner this interview was finished and he could get on the road, the better. Maybe that was why he felt as if he was looking forward to heading home so much. Except that getting to the end of this protracted business of filming didn't explain the frisson of something that was rather more than simply anticipation of an escape. Something that he'd seen in Dexter's face only minutes ago. Something that he hadn't been aware of feeling himself in such a very, very long time.

It felt remarkably like hope...

There was something magic about this place. The stunning view from the suite of rooms that Lady Josephine McKendry occupied in the north-facing upper rooms of the manor house would never get old, Felicity Stephens decided as she took a moment to soak it in. Close to the house, the pebbled pathways were straight lines between neatly trimmed box hedging. Then there were formal gardens and what looked like acres of lawn surrounded by the woodlands that Flick hadn't yet had time to explore, but she could feel the pull towards that fairy tale forest more strongly every time she looked out of these windows.

That echo of Lachlan's voice she heard every time she did so was also gaining strength.

'I guess I know every square inch of this patch of woodlands we own. It's the most beautiful place in the world...'

Was it weird that the pull of that timeless, mysterious woodland in combination with a remembered snatch of conversation could create a twist in her gut that felt like desire? Longing, anyway, although she wasn't sure what it was that was making its absence felt so poignantly. Maybe she was just finally becoming aware of the loneliness that came with her chosen lifestyle.

'What are you looking at, Felicity? You're not getting paid to stand around staring into space, I'll have you know.'

Flick had had two days of practice dealing with Lady Josephine's acerbic comments and had found a strategy that was working well. She simply ignored *what* was being said in favour of trying to interpret *why*.

'Do you need some help getting dressed, Lady Josephine?'

'Don't be ridiculous. I'm not a child.'

The older woman emerged from her en suite bathroom already dressed in what appeared to be her uniform of a tweed skirt, stockings and sensible shoes, a pastel-coloured twinset and a string of pearls. Except that the pearls were still in her hands.

'There's something wrong with the catch,' she said.

'Let me try.' Flick took the necklace, noting the slight tremble in Lady Josephine's hands that was probably why she hadn't been able to fasten the catch. It could also be an early sign of her blood sugar level dropping. Flick bit back a smile. She certainly couldn't rely on irritability being another sign, could she? 'Right...that's got it. Let's test your BGL again.'

'There's nothing wrong with it. I'm not dizzy. I don't have any pins and needles in my hands or feet. And my speech is perfectly coherent.' Lady Josephine walked into her sitting room to sit on an upright chair beside a small table. 'I've had my tablets and my insulin already. I would rather be left alone to get on with my crossword puzzle, thank you.'

'Sometimes it's a good idea to find out if blood sugar levels are falling before you have a full-blown hypoglycaemic episode and end up unconscious on the floor.' Flick wasn't about to be dismissed. She unzipped the small case that held the blood glucose meter, lancets, alcohol wipes and test strips. 'Besides, we talked about this yesterday when your doctor came to visit. It's the new plan designed to see if we can get better control of your diabetes.'

'A plan that's intended to prove I'm incompetent, you mean.' Lady Josephine glared at Flick. 'This is Lachlan's idea, isn't it? He had no right to arrange that doctor's visit behind my back. He wants to see me locked up in some old people's home, doesn't he?'

'Quite the opposite.' Flick held Lady Josephine's finger steady as she pressed the lancet to pierce the skin. Then she used the alcohol wipe again, to discard the first drop of blood that appeared, holding the test strip ready to catch the next drop. 'He wants you to get good control of all your medical issues so that you can get back to things you enjoy. Like walking? Tilly told me that you used to love walking your dog.'

'The dog died,' Lady Josephine snapped. 'And exercise gives me asthma these days, anyway. And angina.'

'It's actually been proven to help strengthen your cardiovascular system. In the long term, it will make it less likely that you'll get attacks of either asthma or angina.'

The chat she'd had with the GP at the end of his visit yesterday had been quite revealing.

'I'm not convinced she does get angina,' he'd told Flick. 'She's refused to have a stress test or even a twelve lead ECG done. It could be asthma but, to be honest, apart from one incident quite a while ago, it's never been severe enough to need anything more than the occasional use of her bronchodilator. I've never needed to put her on steroids. The diabetes is more of a problem but whether it's genuinely brittle or simply the result of poor control or a non-compliant patient is probably something we need to find out.'

Flick made a note of the current reading on the monitor.

'What is it?'

'Just a bit on the high side.'

'So I should have had more insulin. I told you that when we did the test before breakfast.'

'It's not high enough to be a problem,'

Flick said. 'But we're going to test a lot more often for the next few days.' She held on to the monitor. Her next job today was to go through the saved data in the device and see if she could find any patterns. She was going to start a meticulous food diary for Lady Josephine, too. 'Did you understand everything the doctor was saying about it?'

'I'm not an imbecile.'

Flick smiled. 'When I was training, it took me a bit of time to get my head around things like the dawn phenomenon and the re-bound effect that too much insulin can cause and—'

But Lady Josephine was holding up her hand. 'Do stop prattling. Why don't you make yourself useful, instead? Put that dressing gown away and then take that breakfast tray downstairs. Goodness knows what Mrs Tillman's doing but it's obviously not what she's *supposed* to be doing.'

Being a personal servant had never been part of Flick's job description but she wasn't going to let it bother her any more than an unpleasant personality she suspected was a defensive shield Lady Josephine had perfected.

Her dog would have loved her no matter what she was like with people.

How much of a loss had that been?

'I do think we should get some gentle exercise into your daily routine,' she said calmly, as she picked up the discarded dressing gown. 'I can come with you, in my professional capacity, and we can deal with anything that might happen in the way of asthma or angina. I'd love to see more of your gardens.'

'If I want your opinion, I'll ask for it.'

Flick could hear the snappy words coming through the bedroom door but they were easy to ignore as she looked for an appropriate place to hang the dressing gown. It was tempting to leave it on the end of the bed but more intriguing to have a peek into what seemed to be a dressing room beside the bathroom and, when she did, her jaw dropped. Like two sides of a coin, this huge, walk-in wardrobe had an astonishing dividing line. On one side were all the dull skirts and twinsets, sensible shoes and dressy suits. On the other side, muted only slightly by plastic dust covers, was an astonishing number of dresses in every shade of the rainbow. *Ball gowns?*

Still blinking, Flick went back into the sitting room. She opened her mouth to ask about those dresses but Lady Josephine had opened the newspaper to the crossword puzzle page and gave the distinct impression that she would not appreciate being interrupted so Flick changed her mind and picked up the breakfast tray instead.

Timing, she reminded herself, could be everything.

Flick's fork made a loud clatter on the flagstones when she dropped it in surprise at Lachlan's unexpected entrance into the kitchen that evening.

'Sorry… I didn't mean to give you a fright.'

He stooped to pick up the fork at the same time that Flick reached for it, which meant they were suddenly rather too close to each other. At the same moment, they caught each other's gazes and, for a heartbeat, and then another, it seemed that they were both caught—unable to break that contact. He had given her a fright, Flick decided. That was why her heart was beating hard enough to probably be visible. She grabbed the fork and straightened.

'You shouldn't sneak up on me like that,' she told him. 'Next time I might keep hold of my fork and use it to protect myself from intruders.'

He was grinning. 'I'll get you a clean one in that case. May as well cut the infection risk.' He turned away, but not before Flick had discovered it wasn't possible to not return a smile like that.

'I'll get myself one, too,' he said. 'That looks like one of Tilly's exceptionally good shepherd's pies and I'm hungry enough to eat a horse.' He opened a drawer and picked up some fresh cutlery and then got a plate from a cupboard. 'I'm sorry I didn't give you any warning that I was coming. It was a last-minute decision in a crazy-busy day. I'm involved in filming a documentary and it seems to take an inordinate amount of time to rehearse and then film and then do it again if necessary. I've been tripping over cables and having my nose powdered all day.'

Flick accepted the clean fork. She loved eating her dinner, alone at the table, in this gorgeous old kitchen. Mrs Tillman always left something delicious in the oven after taking Lady Josephine's tray to her room, and Flick would come and help herself after she'd written up her notes on her patient, showered and changed out of the tidy skirt, blouse and cardigan she was wearing as a uniform into casual jeans and a soft, comfortable sweatshirt.

The kitchen had instantly become her favourite room of the house and, because it was where she'd shared that dinner with Lachlan on her first night here, it was easy to feel like there was always an echo of him in the room. Having the real thing here, unexpectedly, was taking a bit of getting used to. The kitchen seemed to have suddenly come to life in such a dramatic way that colours seemed brighter. There was more warmth coming from the Aga and even the smell and taste of the food was heightened.

Lachlan had heaped his plate with the savoury mince and its mashed potato topping. Then his chair scraped as he pushed it back on the flagstones and leapt up to stride towards the huge fridge. He had to hunt for a few seconds before coming back with a bottle of tomato sauce.

'Don't tell Tilly,' he said. 'She'd be horrified I still do this. She let me do it when I was a kid but told me never to do it in polite company.'

Flick laughed. 'Who said I was polite?' She reached for the bottle as Lachlan put it down. 'Might just try this myself. I always had a bucket of it to dip my chips into. Hot chips, not crisps,' she added.

'Oh, that's right. Australians are like Americans and call crisps "chips" as well, don't they?'

'Mmm…' Flick shook the bottle and then squeezed it. This was weird, but it felt as if

she'd been sharing food with Lachlan Mc-
Kendry all her life.

And, maybe it was because of that feeling of being so comfortable in his company
that made it seem that they would never run
out of things to talk about, especially when
Flick was genuinely interested in everything
Lachlan was telling her about. Like the documentary that was following children and
teenagers who were facing big physical chal-
lenges.

'When will it be on TV?'

'Not for ages, I expect. They'll need to follow Dexter for at least six months after his
surgery to see how well he learns to use the
new nerves and the amazing difference it
will make to his face…and his life.'

Those last words were so quiet that it
seemed that Lachlan hadn't intended them
to be heard and there was something in his
expression that actually gave Flick a lump
in her throat.

'You know that, don't you? It will make
that much difference.'

Lachlan's face was still now and his gaze was steady. 'It's what I do,' was all he said.

Oh...*wow*...

There was no arrogance in that statement or what it implied. None of the over-confident or superficial gloss that she had assumed went hand in hand with the charm that had put her off when she'd first met Lachlan. That kind of confidence could only come from knowing exactly how good he was at what he did and the unguarded depth Flick could see in those dark eyes made it equally obvious how much he cared about what he did. She'd already had a glimpse of the real person this man was but this...

This was impressive enough to wake up way more than any brain cells. Enough to send a chill down her spine to trickle into every other cell in her body. It was just... incredibly sexy, that was what it was.

And disturbing...because it was an attraction that went deeper than something purely physical.

Flick didn't want to be attracted to Lachlan. She especially didn't want to recognise a soul that was even more attractive than the body that carried it. She hadn't expected to meet someone who could stir feelings like this again. She'd had years of being convinced that her ability to even fall in love had died along with the man she'd considered to be the love of her life. The one she'd chosen to marry and be the father of her children. Any dreams of creating her own family had also been buried back then and it had been a hard-won battle to come to terms with that and find peace with what her life had to offer.

It felt like that peace had just been broken. Like a stone thrown into a still pond, there had been an initial splash and now there were ripples forming. Tiny waves spreading that threatened to undermine the foundations of the new life Flick had created for herself in the last few years.

She didn't dare look directly at Lachlan as he told her that he had lectures and training sessions in the area and that he would be staying in the house for the next few days.

Luckily, she had finished her dinner so she could excuse herself.

'I should go upstairs and see Lady Josephine,' she told him. 'We're doing more frequent BGL measurements and I want to collect her tray and see how much she's eaten. I'm keeping a food diary, which I'll track along with her glucose levels in the hope that we can get better control of her diabetes.'

This was good. Even mentioning Lachlan's mother was enough to create a very safe, professional boundary. Good grief... even acknowledging an attraction to her client's son was just as bad as the way Lachlan had been flirting when he'd found her on his doorstep the other day.

'Sounds good.' Lachlan was reaching for another helping of the shepherd's pie. 'I've got some work I have to get done this evening before my first lecture in Cheltenham tomorrow but please tell her I'll pop in and see her in the morning before I leave.'

'Sure.'

Flick put her plate and cutlery into the dishwasher. She was finding her own control now and it was no problem to find a smile for Lachlan as she left the kitchen. She didn't need to worry about her peace being too disturbed. Ripples from even a boulder being thrown into calm water eventually subsided to leave stillness in their wake again.

She just needed to wait.

Oh…and it might be a good idea to avoid the disruption of anything else like that being thrown in her direction but if it happened again, at least it wouldn't take her by such surprise.

If she was alert, in fact, she might be able to deflect them before they even landed. Because she didn't want to feel those kinds of things. Not again. They were too intense. And, no matter how seductive they might be, they carried the very real danger of being too painful to make them worthwhile.

CHAPTER FOUR

As he'd reminded Tilly when he'd come home to start sorting out the problem with his mother, this kitchen had always been the place Lachlan had found the most homely in the McKendry family's historic manor house. The only place ever that had the magic mix of warmth and welcome and safety, despite anything else that might be happening in the world, that only a real home could provide.

But it was also a place that Lachlan didn't feel like he'd ever quite belonged, no matter how much he would have liked to. Maybe that was because it had never been a place he was supposed to be in. It had been for the cook, when they'd had one, and any other servants employed in the house to help Tilly. He'd never eaten anything other than a treat like a slice of cake or biscuits fresh from the oven at this kitchen table when he'd been a child and the scenario would have been even more unlikely as an adult coming back to visit his parents. The idea of his mother eating in here was unimaginable but that had nothing to do with the reason he'd started avoiding this room himself as he'd got old enough to make his own rules.

No... As Lachlan walked towards the kitchen, having driven up from London again, he was realising that he had probably unconsciously avoided this part of the house for so many years because it tapped into that happy/sad feeling that was so disturbing. A feeling that he'd been aware of more often in the last few days—ever since Felicity Stephens had crashed into his life, come to think of it. And, yes, 'crashed' was an appropriate word because it felt like something had been broken. The thing that had safely contained that feeling, perhaps?

Anyway...it occurred to him now that, if he wanted to fix whatever had been damaged enough to release unwelcome feelings, it might be necessary to find a way to identify exactly what it was, so he thought about it briefly as he passed the sweep of where the main staircase began in line with the doors to the formal drawing room. It was an unsuccessful process, however, because the feeling was too nebulous. Like a fragment of dream being chased after you'd woken up and the closest impression Lachlan could catch was that it felt like seeing the missing thing you'd been searching for forever at the precise moment it was vanishing from sight around a corner.

The happy part came from whatever it was that he'd caught sight of.

The sad part was because it vanished again, leaving a bereft certainty that it could never be captured.

He didn't bother turning his head to look through the door into the formal dining room as he got to the point where the hallway narrowed as it led to the service areas of the house. He'd instinctively known that a meal with Flick at one end of the mahogany table that could seat twenty people would not have helped his quest in persuading her to stay and care for his mother. Tilly's fabulous meal in the comfort of the kitchen, along with that Australian wine, had been perfect—not only because Flick had decided to stay—and that shepherd's pie a couple of nights ago, even though it had been only the second meal he'd ever eaten either in the kitchen or with Flick, had made him feel as if he'd been doing it for ever.

As if...

As if there was a new dimension to what this heart of the house had to offer in the way of being homely.

'Perfect timing,' Flick said as he entered the kitchen. 'You have a knack of arriving when dinner is ready.'

Her welcoming smile only deepened the thought that was still lingering in Lachlan's head. That he'd missed something along the way. That this genuinely *was* home and it had been a mistake to avoid it for so long. He'd eaten out in a prestigious, local restaurant last night with some of the senior doctors from both the Cheltenham Central and Gloucester General hospitals who had invited Lachlan to lead the plastic surgery component of the postgraduate training course being offered and it had been a delicious meal, but he was actually looking forward to Tilly's cooking tonight even more. Like her roast chicken, perhaps?

Or…

'What is that?' He stared at the dish on the table.

'Asparagus quiche.' Flick already had a segment on her plate and she was adding some salad. 'Your mother requested a light dinner and agreed that keeping a food diary is a good incentive to make some healthy changes here and there.' There was a twinkle in those astonishingly blue eyes that made it impossible not to smile at her. 'Although what she actually said was more along the lines of, "I don't suppose I can stop you if you're so determined to be the food and calorie police".' Flick was grinning back at Lachlan. 'Grab a plate. It smells great.'

'Hmm.' Lachlan headed for the cupboard but paused to lift the lid of a crockery bread bin to release the scent of a freshly baked loaf. He was smiling as he put the bread-board, loaf, knife and a big pat of butter onto the table but then he paused again, his smile fading.

'You're…um…wearing a uniform.'

A smart uniform, he had to admit, with what seemed to be a very stylish kind of clinically white tunic with a side fastening of buttons and a softly curved V-neck that was outlined with a dark navy blue that matched her trousers.

'I always do,' Flick told him. 'I hadn't brought it with me when I came here because I packed in a hurry and I wasn't sure I was going to take the position anyway but I've had some of my stuff sent from London so I can look more professional. Your mother approves. I would normally get changed before dinner but I got too hungry.'

Lachlan approved as well because it seemed to signal that Flick was settling into the position and wasn't about to disappear. For a moment, he was tempted to say something along the lines of how much he also approved of women in uniform but he bit that back, knowing how unwelcome it would be. He, too, needed to be professional, he reminded himself as he sat down at the end of the table. He couldn't help another glance at Flick, however, as he sliced off a thick wedge of the bread.

She had her hair scraped back into a pony-tail that was clipped up to the back of her head but there were strands of those blonde waves that were clearly determined to escape and Flick pushed one of them back and tucked it behind her ear as if she was aware of his gaze. Not that she looked up from her plate but just watching that deft movement of her fingers and the odd notion that he could feel that touch himself was enough to make Lachlan search for a distraction.

'How's it going?' he asked. 'With my mother?'

'I think our plan to test her BGL more often and take precise notes of any food intake is paying off. Her levels have been steadier than they have been for a while.'

'That's great.'

'On the other side of the equation, though, I'm not making much progress in the plan to get her exercising more. She hasn't even come downstairs in the few days I've been here already and Tilly tells me she hasn't set foot outside the house in months. And, before that, it was only to take the dog out. I offered to go with her, in case it brings on her asthma or angina, but she…um…wasn't keen on that idea.'

'Bit your head off, huh?' Lachlan shook his head. 'Dogs and biting. It's what I've been talking about all day.'

'Oh?'

'I had a session at a private hospital in Gloucester and one at Cheltenham Central this afternoon. It's postgraduate surgical training that's intended to incorporate plastic surgery techniques into other areas of paediatrics where applicable.'

'But…dogs?'

'Children are the main victims of dog attacks and the injuries can be horrendous. It's not always possible to transfer them to a specialist paediatric trauma centre like my London base at St Bethel's Hospital and, sometimes, the wounds aren't serious enough to warrant that so advanced techniques in debridement and suturing are something all surgeons are keen on learning.'

'I can imagine.'

Flick was holding his gaze now, clearly interested in what he was telling her. Because this was a professional discussion and that gave her permission to let her guard down? Thank goodness he hadn't made some stupid, flirtatious remark about how good she looked in her uniform. As if it made any difference, anyway. Flick would still look gorgeous if she was wearing a sack.

Or nothing at all...

Hastily, Lachlan dropped his gaze to his meal and focused on his food, Until he could sense a growing tension in the air. At least he knew how to defuse that now.

'Dog bites are very challenging injuries for plastic surgeons,' he told Flick. 'And more than half the cases involve the face. A dog doesn't just bite, either—it tends to clamp its jaws and then shake its head. A puncture wound can become a combination of crush, laceration and tear injuries, sometimes with a fracture to complicate things even further.'

Flick's eyes had widened. 'Maybe I won't suggest that we get your mother a new dog, then, to encourage her to exercise.'

Lachlan laughed. 'Our lovely old golden retrievers wouldn't have hurt a fly. Brie was the last one and she got to the grand old age of seventeen. I don't imagine her walks with my mother in recent times would have been exactly strenuous exercise.' He ate a last bite of his quiche. 'She used to be as fit as a fiddle. She was a competitive ballroom dancer in her youth.'

'Oh…that explains the dresses.'

'What dresses?'

'In her wardrobe. I was putting her dressing gown away and one side of the wardrobe is full of amazing-looking dresses. I thought they must be ballgowns but now that I think about it, they were too short for that and it makes sense. Wow…she must have done a lot of dancing.'

'She taught it. That was how she met my father. She came here to give him private lessons in the ballroom, apparently.'

Flick's jaw had dropped. 'You have a *ballroom*?'

'Have you not gone exploring?'

She shook her head but then one side of her mouth curled into a hint of a cheeky grin. 'I wanted to,' she admitted, 'but it felt a bit like snooping. And Tilly said that most of the house is shut up because it's never used and it's too expensive to heat.'

The idea that he could give Flick something that she'd just admitted she wanted was enough to make Lachlan feel inordinately pleased with himself.

'Shut up, maybe, but it's not locked up. Have you had enough to eat?'

'Yes, thanks…why?'

'I'll give you the grand tour.' Lachlan got to his feet.

'Now?'

'Well, having a look at the gardens and the bluebell woods might need to wait for daylight but we have plenty of lights in the house. Unless you've got something else you'd rather be doing?'

'Are you kidding? I'd love to.'

Oh…that *smile*… It didn't just light up a room. It made the entire world a brighter place. It made Lachlan believe that there was joy to be found in the most unexpected places. That simply being in Felicity Stephens' company was a delight and that she would be up for all kinds of adventure. Fun with a capital *F*.

He didn't take her upstairs because that was mainly just bedrooms and bathrooms other than his mother's larger suite that Flick was already familiar with. Going up to the old servants' quarters in the attics would be fun but probably too dusty and potentially badly lit. There was more than enough to show her on the ground floor, anyway, like the formal dining room not far from the kitchen and then the enormous drawing room that had the conservatory at the other end.

There was his father's study that looked as if it hadn't been touched since his death, the library with its leather armchairs and walls of books that actually had the original ladders needed to get to the higher shelves, the gallery with McKendry portraits that went back several hundred years, and finally the ballroom with its magnificent parquet flooring, ornate plaster ceiling and the wall of arched windows that looked out onto the terrace and gardens like the formal drawing room. The chandeliers still glittered despite probably more than a decade of gathered dust and the look on Flick's face was one of absolute awe.

'I feel like I've got a part in some period drama.' She was almost whispering. 'I'm actually wearing a big, boofy dress and, any moment now, the orchestra is going to let rip with something like "The Blue Danube".'

'Classic.' Lachlan smiled.

He walked towards a cabinet near the main doors to the room. 'There was a state-of-the-art sound system installed in here just before my father died. I wonder if it still works after all this time.' He switched it on, watched the chosen disc with its classic waltz music slide into place and then adjusted the volume controls as the first notes of the violins came through the dozens of speakers that had been discreetly placed to provide surround sound that was so good it felt like the room had an invisible, full symphony orchestra in attendance. Seeing the delight on Flick's face, Lachlan turned the volume up a bit more before walking back to her. He twirled his hand, gave a bow and then straightened to offer his hand.

'May I have the pleasure of this dance, Mademoiselle?'

Flick just laughed. 'I can't dance to save myself,' she said.

'And I was required to learn when I was seven years old,' Lachlan responded. 'This will be a good test of how good I still am at leading.'

He could see her hesitating so he held her gaze and hoped that she would understand that this might not be professional but he wasn't hitting on her, he was offering her an insight into who he was. The things that had shaped him into the man he was today. He wanted her to know who he really was, he realised—as a person and not her employer. In the same way that he wanted to get to know who the real Felicity Stephens was and why she chose to live her life in the way she did, without any solid roots in a particular place or lifestyle, which was pretty much the opposite of what Lachlan had always been expected to embrace.

It was unlikely that Flick could read anything below the surface, of course, but whatever it was she saw in his eyes, it was enough to make her shake her head but keep smiling. Even better, it was enough to persuade her to take his hand.

'Okay…put your left hand on the top of my arm, keep hold of my right hand and here we go…' He kept his movements in slow motion as he directed her. 'Step back with your right foot, sideways with your left foot and then close the gap with your right foot.'

There was fierce concentration on Flick's

face as she followed his instructions and she managed to reverse the movements of the basic box step to start by going forward with her left foot. By the time they had repeated the move slowly a few times, it felt like she was getting the hang of it.

It also felt like the warmth of Flick's skin was starting to burn Lachlan's hands. He only had his hand loosely against her back but he was acutely aware of every movement of her muscles and that heat and her softness and it seemed to be seeping into every cell of his own body.

'You're doing great,' he told her. 'Let's see if we can actually do it in time with the music, shall we?'

It wasn't a huge increase in speed but it was enough to confuse Flick completely. She stepped on his toes, used the wrong feet, swore several times and finally started laughing helplessly.

Lachlan was still holding her hand. He still had his other hand on the small of her back but they weren't stepping in any direction. Flick felt like she was melting in his arms as she laughed but then she got control of herself and looked up at him.

'Sorry…but I did warn you…'

'You did.' He was smiling down at her. He wanted to tell her that she didn't need to apologise. That his toes would recover in no time and he'd actually enjoyed this impromptu—albeit unsuccessful—dance lesson.

And then he realised just *how* much he had enjoyed it.

How much he was loving the feel of this woman between his hands.

And time seemed to stop right about then because they were still holding each other's gazes and it was one of those moments that was a tipping point and Lachlan knew exactly which way it could tip. He only needed to see the slightest hint of an invitation and he would be kissing this gorgeous, vibrant woman.

The romantic music was still filling the room but somehow they both heard another sound and it was only then that they both discovered they were being watched. How long had his mother, with her dressing gown tied tightly around her waist, been standing there in the open doors that led to the main hallway of the house?

Shocked, Lachlan moved swiftly to turn off the music. Flick was looking just as shocked, nervous even, as silence fell and rapidly deepened in the wake of the music being cut. It was Flick who had the courage to speak first, however.

'You came downstairs,' she said.

'Obviously,' Lady Josephine snapped. 'Seeing that you didn't answer your pager, I decided I'd have to find out for myself what was going on with all the lights on and that loud music.'

'Oh, no…' Flick looked horrified now. 'I must have left my pager in the kitchen.'

'Sorry, Mother,' Lachlan said.

Had she seen that he'd been seriously thinking about kissing her private nurse? Would that be enough, without the disturbance of the music, to use this as an excuse to fire Flick? That would send him back to square one in his attempt to make life easier for both of them just when he was starting to feel like his life was under better control?

'We didn't mean to disturb you,' he added, his gaze sliding briefly sideways to catch Flick's. 'It won't happen again.'

'You've always managed to create a disturbance without trying,' his mother said. But it was Flick she was staring at. 'You can't dance,' she said. 'I've always considered that an appalling lack in any young woman.'

Flick's huff of breath sounded more amused than incredulous. 'Lachlan tells me that you used to be a dance teacher,' she said. 'Maybe I've come to the right place, then?'

Lady Josephine turned away but Lachlan was quite sure he heard her muttered words.

'Maybe you have.'

It had been a real risk being that cheeky to her client but, at the time, Flick hadn't given it a second thought. As she went after Lady Josephine to offer help in getting back up the stairs, she realised that part of her might have actually been hoping that she would get fired on the spot.

Because she deserved to be?

If they hadn't been interrupted at that point in time, Flick knew that she would have ended up kissing Lachlan McKendry. She might not want to be attracted to this man but wishing it away was never going to work. Worse, in that moment, she'd had the distinct impression that Lachlan was equally attracted to her. And, when he'd looked at her as he'd told his mother that it wasn't going to happen again, she'd also realised that he didn't want anything to be that disturbed—including her role as Lady Josephine's carer.

It had felt like a tacit agreement that, yes, there was attraction there, but nothing was going to happen. And that was fine by her. But Lady Josephine was still obviously highly irritated by the incident, judging by her curt refusal of assistance from Flick and the speed with which she started going up the sweeping staircase. She stopped when she got to the landing, however, and Flick caught up with her as she clutched the bannister with one hand and put the other to the centre of her chest.

'What is it?' Flick asked instantly. 'Are you having trouble breathing?'

'No…it's my chest… Pain…'

Flick took hold of her arm. 'Sit down. Here, on the stairs.'

'What's going on?' Lachlan was walking out of the ballroom and had paused at the foot of the staircase. He came up the stairs two at a time when he saw Flick helping his mother to sit down.

'Chest pain,' she said quietly.

'Show me where,' Lachlan demanded. 'Does it go anywhere else? Like into your arm?'

Lady Josephine shook her head.

'How bad is the pain? On a scale of one to ten with one being no pain and ten being the worst you can think of?'

'…*nine*…'

'Right.' Lachlan scooped his mother into his arms.

'Put me *down*,' she demanded.

'Nope. I'm not about to let you go off to

your room and die from a heart attack. I'm taking you to hospital.' He looked back as he started down the stairs. 'Flick, could you go and grab Mother's GTN spray? And then come with us, please? There's no time to wait for an ambulance to get here from Cheltenham and I'll need someone else in the car.'

He didn't need to say that he might need help if this escalated into something as serious as cardiac arrest. 'Of course.'

'I do *not* want to go to hospital,' Lady Josephine said. 'You can't do this, Lachlan. I won't allow it.'

Lachlan shook his head. 'We're going to get you properly checked this time. And, Flick?'

She paused at the top of the stairs. She could see the real concern in Lachlan's face. There was no way his mother was going to persuade him to let her stay at home and she liked how much he obviously cared.

'What is it?'

'Could we take your car, please? There's not much of a back seat in mine.'

The back seat of the Volkswagen Beetle wasn't that much bigger than Lachlan's sports car but Flick was small enough to be able to sit beside Lady Josephine as they sped towards the nearest hospital. It made more sense for Lachlan to drive, anyway, seeing as he knew these narrow, country roads far better than she did. She kept her fingers on Lady Josephine's pulse, which was a little rapid but steady, and she was watching carefully for any signs of deterioration.

'Has your spray made any difference?'

'No.'

'We'll try another dose in a few minutes, then.' Being unresponsive to the medication could mean that this was more than an episode of angina but Lady Josephine didn't seem to be showing any other signs that she could be suffering a heart attack. Her skin was warm and not clammy and she wasn't unduly distressed.

'You're not feeling like you might be sick, are you?' Flick asked.

'No. I've told you, I don't need to go to

hospital. I'm in my dressing gown, for heaven's sake. How embarrassing is this?'

The triage nurse in the emergency department could see how embarrassed her new patient was. 'You're in exactly the right place, Mrs McKendry. Sorry, Lady McKendry. It's very important to get something like chest pain looked at. We're going to get you into a private cubicle now and get a monitor on to see what's happening to your heart.'

Apparently, there was nothing abnormal happening. Flick was standing at the foot of the bed as the consultant was talking quietly to Lachlan a short time later.

'There's no sign of any ST depression. Or anything else that would concern me on her twelve lead ECG. Your mother's in great shape for her age.'

'But she had chest pain after climbing stairs. She does suffer from angina.'

'I can't see any confirmation of that diagnosis in her notes. She did come in for an asthma attack a while back. Perhaps it's chest tightness that's being interpreted as pain?'

'That's possible.'

'If so, that doesn't seem to be a concern at the moment, either. Her oxygen saturation on room air is normal and she's not showing any signs of respiratory distress, apart from hyperventilating a bit when she first arrived.'

'I'll talk to her,' Lachlan said. 'Or maybe it would be better coming from you. You might be able to persuade her to have a proper investigation, like an exercise stress test.'

'I'll see what I can do. Oh…and thanks again for your lecture today. I found it extremely educational.'

Lady Josephine wasn't about to agree to any investigations. 'I'm absolutely fine. Take me home, Lachlan. Now, thank you.'

A nurse found a wheelchair to take Lady Josephine out to the car. Flick was astonished at the smile she offered Lachlan.

'Good to see you again,' she murmured. 'Give me a call sometime?'

'Friend of yours?' Flick asked as she pushed the wheelchair out of the cubicle. She'd been more than astonished by the blatant flirting of that nurse, if she was honest. She was aware of a nasty little flash of something that felt almost like jealousy.

'Never seen her before in my life.' Lachlan sounded bemused enough to be believable.

They'd parked her car illegally in one of the on-call doctors' car-parking slots in the ambulance bay but, because the consultant had recognised Lachlan as a visiting specialist, nobody had asked for it to be moved.

There was someone else waiting to use the parking slot, though he didn't seem annoyed when he saw Lachlan opening the driver's door.

'Thanks, Josh,' he called. 'No time now but we really need to catch up soon.'

Lachlan shook his head as he shut his door. 'Weird,' he muttered. 'You'd think I'd been working here for years instead of it being my first visit to the ED.'

'First and last as far as I'm concerned,' his mother told him. She lapsed into silence after that for the trip home. She was sitting in the front passenger seat this time and Flick had insisted on being in the back.

'You'd be more squashed than an extra sardine,' she told Lachlan. 'You drive. That way we'll all get home faster. It's getting late and I'm sure your mother's very tired.'

She was tired herself but it only took looking away from the window to catch a glimpse of Lachlan's profile to give Flick the feeling that she wouldn't be falling asleep anytime soon tonight. Not if it was going to be as difficult as she suspected it would be to stop the whirl of thoughts clamouring to take priority in her head. That car crash of a dancing lesson, for example, and how Lachlan had made her laugh so much her knees had almost buckled. When had she last laughed like that?

Too long ago.

She was remembering, too, that look on his face of such deep concern for his mother. He cared so much and it broke her heart that his love did not seem to be reciprocated.

There were deeper thoughts that Flick knew were only waiting for solitude and darkness to surface and take over completely. Like how delicious it had felt to have the touch of Lachlan's hands on her body.

And how disappointing it had been to have been so *almost* kissed…

CHAPTER FIVE

LISTENING TO 'THE BLUE DANUBE' as his silver Porsche ate up the miles between London and Gloucester was a choice that Lachlan would not have believed he would ever make but it was exactly what he needed after the action-packed day yesterday.

For future reference, it was useful to know just how much extra work it was to have a film crew in his operating theatre. It wasn't just the meticulous attention to guarding the sterility of the area, which meant that the cameras needed the same type of plastic covering that was in place on the overhead standing microscope that Lachlan would use for the intricate surgery needed to join nerves. There was also the need to explain every move he was making in layman's terms, even though they would probably only use a small clip of Dexter's actual nerve transfer surgery.

The initial incisions to access both the masseteric nerve and the buccal branch of the facial nerve were probably too gruesome to be seen by a potentially young or non-medical audience. Maybe they would choose to limit the coverage to what could be seen on the large screen that showed the field Lachlan was viewing through the microscope as he used microsutures and fibrin glue to perform the coaptation of the nerve endings. Oh…he had remembered to explain that coaptation meant joining, hadn't he?

Lachlan let the music wash over the need to pick over everything he remembered about the surgery to search for anything he could have done better and he let go of it all after a brief mental review of the visit to Dexter this morning, which had also been filmed. He hadn't forgotten any necessary advice, he decided. He'd warned Dexter to avoid pressure to his cheek, exercise, lifting anything heavy and vigorous tooth brushing. He had his own doctors to watch over him until Lachlan saw him again, which meant he'd been free to move onto his next commitment, which was, coincidentally, another nerve transfer surgery he'd been invited to lead as a teaching demonstration at Gloucester General Hospital.

This afternoon, he was due to meet a team of orthopaedic and neurosurgeons and the head of paediatrics to discuss the case of a young boy who'd been left with nerve damage after breaking his collarbone that was seriously impacting his ability to use his arm.

At least he could use this short journey as a bit of time out. He'd slept well in his apartment last night so it had to have been the extra pressure of performing in front of cameras that had left him feeling so much more tired than usual. The enjoyment of feeling the power and responsiveness of this wonderful vehicle he was driving was also a boost and, with the delightful sound of the classical music surrounding him, Lachlan could indulge for a while in what felt like the happiest place he could have found.

Except that wasn't quite true, was it? This music was reminding him of the sheer pleasure he'd found in having Flick in his arms the other night. A pleasure that he'd known was out of bounds. He hadn't needed his mother's arrival, just in time to make sure he didn't kiss Flick, to remind him of why she was there in the first place—and how desperately he needed her to stay there. The episode of angina, or asthma, or whatever it had been had given them all a bit of a fright but, on the positive side, it seemed that his mother now also realised how lucky they were to have Flick in the house.

Good grief…his mother was actually undertaking to teach Flick how to dance the waltz. Lachlan found himself smiling as he remembered the conversation that had taken place the day after that trip to the emergency department.

'What are you looking like that for, Felicity? It was you that said maybe you'd come to the right place, because you found out I used to teach dance. It was also your idea

that I should be getting some exercise and I'd rather be walking around in the ballroom than outside, getting rained on and dirty shoes.'

'I...um...guess it might be a useful thing to know how to do.'

'It's more than useful. It's simply good manners, as far as I'm concerned. Like knowing how to eat your soup correctly.'

The look Flick had sent in Lachlan's direction at that point had been priceless. She might as well have had a bubble over her head like a cartoon character, saying 'There's a correct way to eat *soup*?'

Oh, yeah... They needed to have Felicity Stephens in that house. It was coming back to life. No... Lachlan couldn't remember it ever having the kind of life that seemed to be taking hold now. The kind that made him wish he'd already completed his afternoon appointment so that he could be heading home right now. Who knew—maybe Flick would encourage his mother to embrace life the way she did herself? To find some happiness, even?

Maybe the suggestion of getting another dog was worth thinking about as well? And if anyone could persuade his mother to take on a challenge like training a new pup, it would be Flick. After all, she'd practically goaded Lady Josephine into giving her dance lessons, hadn't she, and broken the barrier that had kept the older woman in her personal suite of rooms for months.

Lachlan's breath came out in a huff of laughter. How many times had she trodden on his mother's toes already?

No wonder London Locums considered her to be one of their best. Flick was more than simply an excellent nurse, she was capable of not only dealing with difficult patients but making real progress with their health issues. And she was absolutely professional at all times.

Well…almost all times. Perhaps dancing with your employer might be considered less than entirely professional but it wasn't as if she'd kissed him. She knew as well as he did that it would be crossing an unacceptable line.

What would his preferred choice really be, Lachlan mused as he turned off the motorway and took the route his sat nav was advising to get to Gloucester General Hospital—to keep Flick as a professional medical carer for his mother? Or to be free to kiss her senseless?

His sigh was resigned as he completed his journey and had to leave the cocoon of this glorious car and get back to the real world. He would choose both, of course, but, sadly, that wasn't an option.

'Hi,' he heard someone call. 'What are you doing out here?'

Lachlan was turning, his key in his hand so that he could press the control and double-check he'd locked his car. When he turned back, he couldn't see who the woman had been calling to and, oddly, she seemed to be looking at him. Was this going to turn into another one of those weird encounters like the ones he'd had in Cheltenham Central's emergency department the other evening?

'Hey... *Josh...?*'

Apparently it was.

'Oi!' the woman was shouting now. 'What's going on, Josh? Are you seriously just going to walk away from me?'

That did it. He'd had enough. He stopped and turned.

'What is it with people calling me *Josh*?' he demanded. 'It seems to happen every-where I go around here. And who the hell are *you*?'

A very attractive woman, he realised as he spoke. She had wildly curly auburn hair and dark eyes and she looked...well, about as feisty as Flick. But she was nothing like Flick, really, so noting her attraction was purely academic.

'My name's Stevie,' she told him. 'And I'm sorry I shouted at you like that but...but you look incredibly like a friend of mine. Some-one who works here. I...thought he was ig-noring me.'

'Ah...' Lachlan managed to find a hopefully polite smile. 'And this friend is called Josh, I take it?'

'Yes...'

'I'm Lachlan,' he said. 'Lachlan McKendry. If you work here, perhaps you can help? I'm heading for a meeting in the paediatric department.'

'Oh...of course. I've heard about you. You're the famous plastic surgeon.'

A random nurse in the car park knowing who he was was almost as disconcerting as being called by the wrong name. He didn't have the time to waste on something that was making the hairs prickle on the back of his neck, anyway. He turned towards the hospital buildings again.

'Wait...' Stevie sounded hesitant. 'I know this might sound totally crazy but...are you, by any chance, adopted?'

Lachlan could feel his jaw sagging. This was just getting weirder. 'Not that it's any of your business,' he said slowly. 'But, no, I'm not.'

'Sorry...it's just that you look so much like Josh, you could be brothers. Twins, even.'

That made him laugh but then he shook his head. 'Sounds like the stuff of fairy tales. If you'll excuse me, I don't want to be late for my meeting.'

'I know exactly where you need to be,' Stevie said. 'Follow me.'

She led him rapidly through hospital corridors and up flights of stairs but when she finally opened a door and held it for him, he found himself somewhere he couldn't have dreamed of expecting. He was on the roof of the hospital. This was getting beyond weird.

'What's going on…?'

'Wait here.' Stevie's voice suggested he would be wise to do what he was told. 'Trust me, please…there's someone you have to meet before you do anything else. He's the head of the paediatric department so it's who you've come here to see anyway, but…' She shook her head as though it was going to take too much time to explain. 'I'll be back in a few minutes and then you'll understand why this is so important.'

He could have simply ignored her instruction, followed her back into the stairwell and found his own way to the paediatric department but…there was something in her tone and body language that made him feel curiously on edge. As if something major was about to happen in his life. If nothing else, a few minutes in the fresh air might let him regain his balance and, as far as hospital roofs went, this was an interesting place. It seemed to have been taken over by raised garden beds that looked like they were full of vegetables. Some of the planters had sizeable trees in them and there were seats dotted around, giving the impression that this might be a place that hospital staff came for some time out. To have lunch, maybe?

He was still admiring the layout when Stevie reappeared with someone following her.

That was when weird became spooky.

Lachlan was watching a mirror image of himself walking towards him. Same height. Same hair. Same *nose*…

'Josh?' Stevie was looking up at her companion. 'This is Lachlan McKendry. Lachlan, this is Josh Stanmore. Um… I thought it might be a good idea if you two had a bit of time before your meeting.'

Lachlan couldn't say anything. Neither, apparently, could Josh, until he responded to Stevie asking whether he wanted her to stay. Seconds later, they were alone, still staring at each other, and Lachlan had the impression that Josh knew exactly how he was feeling. That maybe his world was spinning off its axis enough to make him feel that he was about to fall.

'Come…let's sit down.'

They went to one of the wooden benches between the gardens, sat down and then stared at each other again. As strangers, it should have been incredibly rude. Instead, it felt as natural as breathing.

'Where were you born?' Josh asked.

'Cheltenham.'

'Me, too. When?'

Lachlan named the year and month and day of his birth and watched colour drain from Josh's face. His words were no more than a whisper.

'Same…'

'I don't understand.'

'I think I might.' Josh closed his eyes and took a deep breath. 'I'm adopted.'

'But I'm not.' Lachlan shook his head. 'Why would my mother have given one of her babies up for adoption? My father told me once that they'd been trying to have a baby for years. That he was the happiest man in the world to finally have a son and heir. My mother would have done anything to keep him happy and surely giving him *two* sons would have been even better?' His head was spinning even faster now. 'The only way it could make sense was if she didn't know.'

Josh frowned. 'I don't understand. How could she not know she was pregnant with twins? They had pre-natal medicine and ul-trasound back then.'

'Maybe she was told one of her twins had died. Maybe somebody *stole* you.'

Lachlan knew he was staring again but this was beyond huge. He had a *brother*. He could have had a companion for the whole of that long and lonely childhood. Someone to share the fear of being sent away to boarding school. Someone to help him build those secret places in the woods. Someone who could have made everything so much better. He had a lump in his throat that was impossible to swallow and his voice was raw.

'I'll find out,' he promised. He pulled his phone from his pocket. 'Give me your number and I'll get in touch as soon as I can.'

'Let's meet again.' Josh nodded. 'But not here. I'll give you my address as well. This is going to break the hospital grapevine as far as gossip goes so we'll need to decide how we're going to handle it.'

'But we have a meeting.' Lachlan checked his watch. 'It should have started five minutes ago.'

'I'll go and postpone it. Toby's surgery isn't urgent and I doubt that either of us would be able to focus right now so it would be a complete waste of time for everybody involved.'

It took only a minute to exchange details.

'Can you find your own way out?' Josh asked. 'It might be better if we're not seen together yet.'

'Agreed. It was lucky your girlfriend found me in the car park and brought me up here.'

'Stevie's just a good friend,' Josh said. 'But you're right. She's bought us some private time to get a handle on this and find out what actually happened. I guess your mother might be the only one who knows the truth.'

Lachlan could hear the grim note in his own voice. 'We'll soon find out.'

'One-forty over ninety.' Flick removed the earpieces of her stethoscope and hooked it around her neck. 'That's not bad, Lady Josephine. Your GP will be pleased to hear that your blood pressure's down a bit. Now, it's nearly time to check your blood sugar and—'

The interruption as the door of the sitting room burst open without warning gave both women a fright. Flick's immediate concern was for her patient's blood pressure but then she turned towards the door and that changed into concern for Lachlan.

He looked nothing like the confident man who was in control of his world that she'd met on the doorstep when she'd arrived at this house but it wasn't that she was getting a glimpse of the man who was hidden beneath that image. Or maybe she was. This was Lachlan upset. Thrown off balance for some reason and…angry? His words were measured but, yes…they were coming from a place that was raw.

'I want…the *truth*…'

It was probably only Flick who could hear the raggedness of the breath that Lady Josephine sucked in. It was hardly surprising that the automatic defence of being acerbic was used.

'What on earth are you talking about, Lachlan? And what do you think you're doing, coming in here without being polite enough to even knock? The truth about *what*, exactly?'

'About why you let someone steal my brother.'

It was Flick who gasped this time. The other two people in the room were completely silent as they stared at each other. She shouldn't be here, Flick thought, in the middle of what was obviously a private family matter. But what if emotional stress was enough to bring on an asthma or angina attack for the woman whose health was her responsibility?

'Or was it something more than that?' Lachlan broke the silence. 'Did you give one of your babies away because you didn't want twins? Put him up for adoption?'

'Go away, Lachlan. I have absolutely no idea what you're talking about.'

'I should go...' Flick said quietly.

'Stay where you are,' Lady Josephine ordered. 'And find my spray.' She put her hand on the middle of her chest as if she could feel pain.

If she was, it wasn't about to distract Lachlan.

'I met him today,' he said.

Flick could see the muscles in his neck move as he swallowed hard and she realised that Lady Josephine wasn't the only person she was worried about here. Lachlan was grappling with something so huge he was having trouble finding where to start. She wanted to go and stand beside him and offer support.

To hold his hand…?

'His name's Josh Stanmore,' Lachlan continued. 'Born in Cheltenham. On exactly the same day as me, but even before he told me that, there was no mistaking that we were twins. Probably identical twins. It was like… like meeting myself…'

No wonder he was looking so shocked, Flick thought. Her gaze sought the small red cannister that held the GTN spray, in case Lady Josephine's chest pain was genuine. It was on the medication tray beside the asthma inhaler.

'He told me he was adopted,' Lachlan added. 'But he'd never known he had a twin.'

'You can't blame me,' Lady Josephine snapped. 'I wasn't told it was twins.'

'I don't believe you,' Lachlan said. 'You must have known you were pregnant with more than one baby.'

'Oh, for heaven's sake, Lachlan. You're being dense.' His mother looked away, as if the view outside was of more interest. 'I was never pregnant. You were also adopted.'

The silence this time was so deep Flick felt like she was falling into it. How appalling was this? She knew how much Lachlan cared about his mother. And he was only now finding out that she wasn't the woman who'd given birth to him? How much worse could this be?

Quite a lot, it seemed.

'Even if I had known it was twins, I wouldn't have taken you both.' Lady Josephine's voice rose. 'I didn't want *one* baby, let alone two. I only agreed to the adoption because I knew it was the only way to save my marriage. Your father wanted an heir much more than he wanted *me*.'

The sound Lady Josephine made as she dragged in a new breath could almost have been the start of a sob. It could also be the first sign of respiratory distress. Flick watched as another breath was taken, a shorter gasp this time, and she could definitely hear a wheezing sound. She stepped towards the tray and picked up the inhaler but her gaze shifted to Lachlan as she did so. She wanted him to know that she understood how awful this was for him to hear and that, if she didn't feel so incredibly helpless, she would do whatever she could to try and ease *his* pain.

He caught her gaze but not for long enough for any silent message to be exchanged. He stared at his mother again and, for a horrible moment, he looked like a small boy who was fighting not to burst into tears and a piece of Flick's heart broke at that point. She couldn't do anything about it, however. Lady Josephine was definitely having trouble breathing now and she was reaching towards the inhaler Flick had in her hand. She shook the cannister, took the cap off and held it to the older woman's lips.

'Let all your breath out,' she instructed. 'I'll press the button when you start breathing in.'

She didn't see Lachlan leaving the room. She just heard the door slam shut behind him.

A minute later, though, she saw him again

as a movement outside caught her peripheral vision. Lachlan was walking fast, heading towards the woodland that surrounded the garden. The squeeze on Flick's heart made her aware of just how worried she was for him. How lonely was it going to be for him trying to get his head around what he'd just learned?

But she had to turn back to the person she was employed to care for.

'That sounds better,' she said. 'But try and slow your breathing down. Like this…' She modelled taking a slow inward breath and then releasing it again. 'I'll count for you. Take a breath in—one…two…three… And now out again—one…two…three…'

Another glance through the window showed that Lachlan had vanished, presumably into the trees, and Flick's heart sank a little further. It wasn't that long before it would start getting dark, and he hadn't even put a warm coat on…

CHAPTER SIX

'HE'LL BE ALL RIGHT, lovey. He knows those woods like the back of his hand.'

'But it's dark. And cold.'

'I know.' Mrs Tillman wiped her hands on her apron as she sighed heavily. 'Such goings on. This was never the happiest house but this...this feels very different.' She headed back towards the oven. She was cooking Lachlan's favourite dinner of roast beef and Yorkshire pudding because she'd told Flick she didn't know what else she could do to try and help.

'Did you know he was adopted?' Flick asked.

Mrs Tillman shook her head. 'He was a toddler when me and Jack started work here. Maybe two years old? He had a string of nannies. I think Lady J. found a reason to

get rid of them as soon as she knew her husband had started sleeping with them.'

'Oh, no...'

'How is Her Ladyship now?'

'She's upset. It took a while to get her
asthma under control but it was definitely
an emotionally triggered attack. I think
she's telling the truth about not knowing that Lachlan was a twin but... I don't
know, it might have been better *not* to tell
the truth about never wanting a child in the
first place.'

'Aye...' Mrs Tillman sighed again. 'I'll
take her up some dinner, though I don't expect she's hungry. Are you going to have
something?'

'Later. I'll wait until Lachlan comes back.
If he comes back...'

'He'll come back. He always did when he
was a boy and got hungry enough. At least
you'll be here when he does. I need to go
and look after my Jack.'

'Of course. I can take Lady Josephine's
dinner up, if you like.'

'Oh, thank you. To be honest, I'd like to be with my Jack right now.'

Mrs Tillman had been right in thinking that the food wouldn't be welcome, however.

'You need to eat,' Flick told Lady Josephine. 'Or it will be more difficult to control your blood sugar levels. I'll leave it here and come back later for a test.'

Sure enough, she found that Lady Josephine's BGL had dropped when she went back to find the dinner untouched. The insulin dose had to be adjusted and Flick wanted to check again before her patient retired for the night but she was told to go away and not to come back till morning so she had to hope that the pager would be used if she was needed before then.

What was more of a worry was that Lachlan still hadn't returned to the house. Flick found herself pacing and then standing to stare out of whatever windows she could find that gave her a view of the gardens and that ominously dark woodland beyond. Finally, just after nine p.m., she saw the shadowy figure crossing the lawn and then heard the front door slam shut.

By the time she headed for the stairs, having wavered but then decided in favour of intruding at such a personal time, she heard another door slamming shut and knew it was Lachlan's bedroom on the other side of the first floor but Flick wasn't going to let that derail her decision. Instead, she headed for the kitchen, where the oven had long since been turned off.

It wasn't going to be hot roast beef and all the trimmings but the relief that Lachlan was safely back in the house was enough to make Flick realise she needed food and surely he did as well. She cut and buttered thick slices of homemade bread and made sandwiches with the beef. She looked at a jar of horseradish sauce in the fridge, which would have been a classic condiment for the beef, but then she spotted something else and, for the first time in hours, felt her lips curl in a tiny smile. She put a bottle of wine on the tray and then two glasses, which was possibly presumptuous but she'd made enough sandwiches for two people because, even if Lachlan didn't want to talk, it could make a big difference just having some company.

Knowing that someone cared...

The knock on his door was unexpected.

Unwelcome.

But surely his mother hadn't come to hurl any more verbal bombs about how he hadn't been wanted and had never actually belonged here?

'It's only me...'

The sound of Flick's voice through the door was almost equally unsettling because, for a horrible moment, Lachlan felt like he might really lose control and start crying or something. Because he could feel the edges of *that* feeling again—the happy/sad one— but this time it was the happy that was tipping the balance and, man...he could do with a hint of happy at the moment.

He opened the door to find Flick holding a huge tray, laden with plates and wine and...two glasses? It looked heavy and it was automatic to offer assistance by holding his hands out to take the tray. Flick seemed happy to let him take it, following him into his room as if it was an invitation to join him.

'I finally got hungry,' she told him. 'And I figured you'd be even hungrier after tramping around the countryside so I thought we could have a bit of a picnic.'

A picnic? A happy, summery sort of thing to do? The idea was crazy but it also made Lachlan almost smile as he put the tray down on a table near the windows.

'It's freezing in here.' Flick rubbed her arms and then stepped closer to the ornate fireplace on the other side of the room. 'Is it safe to light this?'

'I would think so. Tilly's husband looks after getting chimneys swept every year and it always used to be laid with kindling and a supply of wood every time I came home…came *here*,' he corrected himself. 'I can hardly call it "home" any more, can I?'

Flick ignored his bitter comment. She knelt in front of the fire, striking a match to ignite the screwed-up newspaper beneath the kindling. She wasn't wearing her uniform now, or even the smart clothes she'd worn when she'd first come here. She had well-worn denim jeans on and a white shirt beneath a navy-blue cardigan that looked thick enough to be soft and warm. And… Lachlan took another look…

'What on earth have you got on your feet?'

'Ugg boots.' Flick didn't move, other than to blow on the baby flames to encourage their growth. 'They're an Aussie thing. Lined with sheepskin so they're perfect for English weather almost all year round but especially tonight.' She looked up at him. 'You must be freezing—you went out hours ago and you weren't even wearing a coat.'

The fact that she'd noticed what he'd been wearing, had watched him perhaps and then been worried about him, made something tighten hard in Lachlan's chest, even though he knew it wasn't physically possible for a heart to be squeezed. He was cold right through to his bones, though, he had to admit, so he crouched down beside Flick and held his hands out to the now cheerful flicker of flames.

'This is excellent. We can have our picnic right here.' Flick's smile was even more warming than those flames. 'No, don't move... I'll get the tray.'

She jumped up to fetch the tray before Lachlan could argue but he didn't want to move anyway. There was something very comforting about settling down properly on the hearth rug to watch the flicker of flames and soak in the warmth. Flick put the tray on the rug in front of him and then gathered some cushions from the nearby armchairs.

'Luxury,' she declared with a grin. 'Now, dig in.' She held the plate of chunky sandwiches towards him. 'I'll sort the wine. Also Australian...like my Ugg boots.'

Lachlan hadn't given food a thought as he'd roamed the woodland, trying to deal with an impossible maelstrom of thoughts and emotions, but as soon as he was holding that soft, fresh bread in his hands and got a whiff of the roast beef, he was suddenly starving. One bite in and he found he was having another one of those moments when it felt like tears were embarrassingly close.

'Tomato sauce…?'

'Mmm…' Flick passed him a glass of wine. And a smile. 'A bucket of it.' Her smile widened. 'Hey…it could be considered fine dining from where I come from and…and I knew you liked it.'

The navy blue of the cardigan Flick was wearing was pretty much the same colour as her eyes in the shadows caused by the flickering flames and the firelight was also making streaks in her blonde hair glow like sunshine, but it wasn't this woman's extraordinary beauty that was overwhelming Lachlan right now. It was because she was caring for him. And about him. And she knew the worst, because she'd been right there when he'd learned that horrible truth about the lie his life had been.

The comfort of the fire and food was helping as well. And the wine. Even more, it was that he could feel so comfortable simply being in the company of another person, without needing to make conversation or do anything other than exchange an occasional glance or half-smile.

'I'll get rid of the tray,' Flick offered, when they'd cleared the plates and polished off the wine.

'No...don't move.' The smile Lachlan received told him that Flick was well aware he was echoing her earlier order to him. 'It's... um...nice to have someone to talk to.' Although he hadn't exactly done much talking, what he could see in Flick's eyes told him that she was ready to listen if he wanted to. And...maybe she was the only person in the world he *could* talk to right now. 'I think the occasion calls for dessert,' he added, hurriedly. 'How 'bout I find some ice cream?'

'A picnic wouldn't be complete without it.' Flick nodded.

'And, I don't know about you, but I suspect a day like today also calls for some more wine.'

Flick's nod was grave this time. 'I think so, too,' she murmured. Her gaze was still holding his. 'I'll just stay nice and warm here, shall I?'

'I think that's only fair. It was you who came up with the idea of the picnic, after all.' Lachlan took the wineglasses off the tray and put them down on the tiled hearth. 'I'll be right back.'

Flick could—and probably should—have gone to check on Lachlan's mother and do another blood glucose test but she knew she wouldn't be welcome and she was confident that the pager alarm would be used if something serious happened because that asthma attack today had been genuinely frightening for Lady Josephine. She also knew that Lachlan needed her more right now. Not that he'd said anything about what had happened but that comment he'd made about it being nice to have someone to talk to made her feel the need to hang around a bit longer in case he *did* want to talk about it.

Thank goodness he was, at least, looking a little better after some food and warmth. He'd looked like a ghost when she'd arrived in this room and Flick had had to fight the urge to simply put the tray on the floor and take him into her arms and hold him tightly for as long as it took to start fixing what had been broken. Getting the fire going had been a welcome distraction to fighting that surprisingly powerful desire. Flick added another log or two to tap into the distraction that movement could provide but it didn't stop a distinct feeling of pleasure rippling through her body as Lachlan returned and closed his bedroom door behind him.

He'd been quick because he hadn't stopped to do anything other than collect the basic supplies. He held a tub of ice cream and two spoons in one hand and a bottle of red wine and a corkscrew in the other. Chocolate fudge ice cream, Flick noted as she peeled off the covering, which would be even more delicious with the rich, red wine Lachlan was opening.

There was something disconcertingly intimate about sharing the same tub of ice cream, taking turns to dip their spoons into the treat but sometimes mistiming it enough for the spoons to touch—which felt remarkably like it was their hands touching. Maybe that was what made Lachlan feel like he could finally talk about it.

'So many things make sense now,' he said quietly. 'I knew from very early on that I had to do well at everything I tried because that was what my father noticed. An achievement or a school prize was when I would get hugged. Or be given whatever it was I had my heart set on. He gave me my first Porsche when I was made Dux in my last year at secondary school.'

'This is the boarding school you got sent to when you were only five years old?' Flick could feel the echo of her horror the first time he'd told her about that. She put her spoon down, having lost her appetite for dessert.

Lachlan shrugged. 'I wasn't the only kid that age.'

'But it must have been terrifying. And lonely.'

'Home was pretty lonely, too,' Lachlan said quietly. 'I think I knew all along that my mother didn't love me. I don't think she even liked me so it's no real surprise to learn that she didn't want me. I tried so hard but nothing ever made her really happy. She'd pretend she liked a picture I'd drawn for her, or the bluebells I'd picked in the woods but they disappeared instantly. I think she threw them away the minute I got taken away by my nanny.' He let his breath out in an ironic-sounding huff. 'They are just starting to come out again, those bluebells. Don't think I'll be picking any for Mother *this* year.'

He abandoned his spoon now to pick up his glass and empty it. When he picked up the bottle and offered Flick a refill as well, she simply nodded. She didn't trust herself to speak at the moment in case she interrupted Lachlan's thoughts by doing something stupid, like crying.

'I did a lot of thinking out there tonight,' he said. 'To be honest, it was more of a bombshell meeting Josh today than to finally find out that I was adopted.'

'I'll bet.' Flick was actually reaching out to take his hand before she realised what she was doing. She disguised the movement by shifting the unwanted ice-cream tub to the hearth. 'I can't imagine what it must have been like.'

'It was unnerving,' Lachlan admitted. 'Like looking into a slightly distorted mirror. Our voices sound exactly the same too and...and there was a moment when we both rubbed our forehead at exactly the same time...like this...' He used his middle finger to rub the centre of his hairline and he smiled wryly. 'We even used the same finger...'

'Wow...'

'And out there in the woods, I thought about how much fun we could have had as kids, building the secret places I made alone. I even went and sat in one for a while today. And I thought about how much better school would have been if I'd had someone to share it with. A brother. A *twin*. A best friend...'

'Oh... Lachlan...' This time Flick didn't stop herself from touching his hand. She wrapped her fingers around his and squeezed.

'I feel like I've had half of my life stolen. Half of myself, even. Is that a bit mad?'

'No…' Flick held his gaze. 'No, it's not.'

'I can't forgive my mother. Not that she *is* my mother.'

'If it's any comfort, she really didn't know that you were a twin. She was very upset.'

'She knew she never loved me.' Lachlan's voice was no more than a whisper. 'Or wanted me.'

Again, he drained the rest of his wine from his glass. Then he stared into the fire, which had burnt down to embers. Flick let go of his hand to lean forward and put another piece of wood into the fireplace and it was when she turned back that she saw a single tear rolling down Lachlan's face. Startled, she raised her gaze to catch his and she knew that she was seeing everything there was to see about Lachlan McKendry in that moment.

A man who was completely raw. Being torn apart by incredibly powerful emotions. And Flick knew, only too well, how devastating that could be. She moved quietly, close enough to put her arms around Lachlan because…well…because she needed to hold him as much as she suspected he needed to be held by another human.

Oh…the warmth of her.

The softness.

The murmur of her voice, even though the words made no sense.

He'd never let a woman see him cry. Ever. But she wasn't offering him pity. What he could feel in that embrace was the empathy of someone who understood this depth of pain. Someone who could see past anything superficial to what was important. Someone who could offer love because she had a heart that was as beautiful and real and unique as the rest of her.

Lachlan had no idea when it was that it tipped into something very different.

Escape?

A desire to abandon boundaries that had been put in place to protect a person who'd never felt any desire to protect him?

Or was it simply a surrender to an attraction that had been simmering from the first moment he'd laid eyes on Felicity Stephens and had only been fuelled beyond control by the intimacy of what had happened here this evening? In his bedroom, of all places, with the romance of flickering firelight and the probably unwise addition of a little too much alcohol.

Whatever the cause, it was happening. He'd raised his face from where it had been buried against Flick's shoulder and they were so close to each other their noses were merely a hair's breadth from touching. It could have been Flick who moved first— except it felt like she was melting rather than moving—and he moved his hand to cup her neck for support and then they were gazing at each other for a long, long moment as their breathing mingled and the only sound was the soft crackle of the fire. Silent questions were being asked and answered in that moment.

Do you want this as much as I do?
Yes...oh, God...yes...
We probably shouldn't...
Being professional was a big thing for

Flick. He didn't want her doing something she might regret later.

It's one night...a night like no other will ever be... Maybe we both need it...

That was invitation enough to convince Lachlan. The feeling that maybe his distress had taken Flick back to a place where she had been in need of the kind of comfort she had unhesitatingly offered to him. And that, maybe, she hadn't had somebody there for her?

Whatever...

In slow motion, Lachlan brushed Flick's lips with his own—no more than a butterfly kiss. He saw her eyes close when he did it again and then he closed his own eyes as he let his lips settle against hers, gently feeling the shape of them, angling his head so that his mouth could capture more of that softness and heat that was enough to be spreading through his entire body. And then her lips opened beneath his and he could *taste* her and nothing on earth had ever cast a spell like this and desire became an almost desperate need as he deepened that kiss and let his tongue ask for permission to fulfil more of that need.

Minutes later, they were both fumbling with buttons. His shirt was undone a lot faster than his fingers could manage the tiny buttons on Flick's shirt but there was skin exposed to the firelight in a very short time and he'd never seen anything as enticing as the soft swell of the most perfect breasts in the world. Lachlan lost the power of rational thought as he hooked the edge of her bra to put his lips to that satin skin and his tongue to a nipple that was as hard as a stone. As hard as part of his own anatomy had already become. The tiny sound of need that came from Flick as he undid the fastening of her jeans was almost too much. He had to slow this down or something that was this good would be over too soon when it should last for ever, which was what this perfect woman deserved.

But as he moved to take a breath Flick reached for him to open the zip on his trousers and she was touching him through the fabric, and it was clear that she didn't want this to slow down. Lachlan got to his knees and then his feet. He reached a hand out to Flick who took it, keeping her gaze locked on his as she did so. He pulled her to her feet but only let go to scoop her body into his arms. Then he turned and walked the few steps it took to get to his bed. He set Flick down gently onto her feet and took his sweet time to kiss her again. And then she stood there, completely still, as he carefully removed the rest of her clothing.

She was watching him as he couldn't resist a long look at her body, from head to toe and back again, but, unlike the first time he'd done that, this time she didn't seem to mind at all. She was waiting to capture his gaze as it returned to her face and there was the hint of a smile on her lips.

'Your turn,' she whispered...

CHAPTER SEVEN

'YOU LOOK ABOUT as good as Lady J. does this morning.' Mrs Tillman was frowning as she looked up to see who was coming into the kitchen. 'And that's not a compliment, by the way. Coffee?'

'Oh, yes, please. I might need the whole pot. I didn't get much sleep last night.'

Flick combed her hair back with her fingers and then wound a band around the short ponytail she'd created as Mrs Tillman got milk from the fridge and a mug from a hook. She was hoping there was no hint showing on her face of *why* she hadn't slept much. She had crept back to her own room at some point before dawn and had even drifted into sleep for a brief period before the alarm on her phone had sounded.

Then she'd tapped the snooze function button on the screen at least twice. Not because she wanted to snatch a few minutes' more sleep but because she wanted to remember why her body felt like this. Revel in it, even. In that almost bruised feeling in places that hadn't been touched for so long they had been forgotten but the border between pain and pleasure was too blurred to define.

She was also weary in a way that wasn't due to a lack of sleep but the aftermath of the release of a surprising amount of tension that she hadn't even known she was living with. Probably because it had simply become part of her way of life. One of those things you learned to accept because they couldn't be changed.

Mrs Tillman put a mug of fragrant coffee in front of Flick and then shook her head.

'It's rattled everybody, this business. I saw young Lachlan out walking as soon as dawn broke.'

'Oh?' Flick couldn't control the sudden jump in her heart rate but she could crush that inappropriately fierce flash of disappointment. 'He's already had breakfast, then?'

What had she been expecting—that he would be waiting to see her? That she'd know, just by looking at him, that last night had been more meaningful than simply a one-off escape from overwhelming emotional upheaval? How ridiculous. It wasn't as if she would even want that to be the case.

'He said he'd pick something up later. He's back to London for the day.' Mrs Tillman was back at the sink, reaching for something on the windowsill. 'He left this for you. Maybe he knew you wouldn't have had a great night either.'

It was a small jam jar she was holding, with a tiny bunch of flowers in it.

'Or maybe he's scared that you won't want to hang around and work for Lady J. any longer with the family skeletons coming out. That he'll come home and find that you've packed your bags.'

'I'd never leave someone in the lurch, even if I did want to change positions.' But the idea that Lachlan was worried she might disappear made Flick smile as she buried her nose in the blooms. 'I love bluebells,' she said. 'They smell like the woods. And spring. And…'

And these ones made her realise that Lachlan had been thinking about her at the same time she had been lying in her bed, thinking about him. He'd given her something that had meaning, too, because he'd told her that he'd given his mother bunches of bluebells to try and win her love but she'd thrown them away. Flick was not going to throw these away.

'I'll take these to my room when I go upstairs,' she said aloud. Maybe she knew what else these flowers smelled of now. The start of something new? Not that she had any idea of what that something might be but she was again aware of how different her body felt this morning. That was certainly new.

And it was…unexpectedly nice…

More than nice. Lachlan was probably halfway to London already but this feeling gave her a connection that was not about to break, even if it was being stretched over that kind of considerable distance.

'I'd better head up now, in fact,' she added,

picking up her coffee as well as the jam jar. 'I'm a bit worried that you think Lady Josephine's not looking well.'

He didn't really have anything urgent enough to require a trip to London but the pull towards St Bethel's Hospital and the Richmond International Clinic was too strong to ignore. Maybe he needed to reconnect with the life he'd had only days ago, before it had been turned inside out. Some time in his modern apartment with the stunning view over the Thames would also make a welcome change from the sombre stone walls of his ancient family home and the woodland that surrounded it.

Family home…as if…

There was still a pull from that direction, though. Lachlan could feel it even as he soaked in the feeling of power beneath his hands and played with the boundaries of the permitted speed limits as he passed every other vehicle on the motorway. It was raining but his automatic wipers were maintaining perfect visibility and the way the car was stuck to the road with its built-in safety features gave him the confidence to push just a little further. The adrenaline rush was almost enough to banish the fatigue that was only to be expected after a totally sleepless night.

The tug of that pull to the house he'd left behind him was suddenly sharp and it was centred deep in his gut and...and it felt like desire.

Was that what this pull was all about? Flick...and the most amazing sex he'd ever had in his life?

It wasn't clear cut, though, was it? Their night together had been in his childhood home and it had only happened because he'd been completely thrown off balance by what had happened yesterday. To find he had a brother. To learn that his mother had never wanted him. It was no wonder that he'd sought comfort in someone's arms and the chance to escape reality briefly.

That didn't explain why he'd been drawn

to the woods at first light this morning, mind you. Or why he'd searched through the swathe of flowers to find the few that were open enough to give the scent he remembered so well from his childhood. Why had he wanted to do that so much? He'd told Flick the flowers had been one of the unwanted gifts he had given his mother. Was he so confident that she would understand that he was trying to thank her for her understanding? For being there? That she would recognise the symbol for what it was?

Yes...he was that confident. Nobody had ever touched him quite like that in his life—both physically and emotionally.

Felicity Stephens was an extraordinary woman. She might not be in his life for very long but he had to thank his lucky stars that she'd happened to be there last night, when he'd needed someone so badly. Not just anyone, either. Lachlan was quite sure that nobody else on earth could have made him feel like she had. As though he was truly worth caring about. As though *she* cared that much…

The text message on his phone came onto the dashboard screen as Lachlan slowed for the first set of traffic lights on the outskirts of the city.

Josh here. Don't know about you but I didn't get much sleep. How 'bout we meet again tonight? Here's my address—

Another great feature of this new car was the ability to answer a text verbally.

'Sure thing,' Lachlan dictated. 'I'm in the City for the day but should be back by seven p.m. See you then.'

Looking up from the screen, he caught a glimpse of the top of his face in the rear-view mirror. Good grief…how could he look this wrecked with just one night's sleep missed? The skin around the bottom of his eyes looked blue enough to be bruised—as if he'd been in some kind of fight.

How battered his spirit felt matched that notion as well, come to think of it.

It didn't occur to him to send a message to Tilly to let her know he wouldn't be back for dinner. Maybe he didn't want his mother to know where he was. It wasn't simply that it was none of her business. He didn't want the reminder that she didn't actually care—because she never had…

The rain had set in by early afternoon.

Lady Josephine looked as tired as Flick was feeling and she was in a very strange mood. Even one of her cutting comments would be preferable to the awful silence that filled the room as Flick went through the routine of checking and recording vital sign measurements. With the weather making the room as dingy and dismal as the atmosphere, it was obvious that something had to be done.

'Would you like me to bring you up some afternoon tea? And light the fire, perhaps?' Oh, that suggestion might not have been the best. It reminded Flick instantly of lighting the fire in Lachlan's room last night. And everything that had followed…

She cleared her throat. 'It's a bit of a dull afternoon, isn't it?' she added hastily.

Lady Josephine snorted. 'I thought it was a uniquely English attribute to resort to talking about the weather to avoid anything more awkward.'

Something in her tone suggested that she would rather be talking about the awkward things and Flick hesitated only a moment before putting both of her suggestions into action. Carrying the tray up from the kitchen a short time later, she was confident she was doing the right thing. Okay, the family's private business was not something she should get into, but it was affecting her patient enough to have potentially serious consequences—like that asthma attack yesterday—so, if Lady Josephine wanted to talk, it was actually part of Flick's job to listen.

Preferably without judgement, she reminded herself as she poured the tea and buttered one of Mrs Tillman's excellent cheese scones, although that might prove difficult. This involved Lachlan, after all, and she had shared his heartbreak yesterday in a way that made her far more involved than was strictly professional.

Professional boundaries didn't seem to be concerning Lady Josephine, either.

'I've been thinking,' she announced as Flick offered her the milk jug. 'You're about the size I used to be at your age. I'm too scrawny now, of course.'

'For what?'

'To wear my dresses.' Lady Josephine took a sip of her tea but pushed the plate with the scone aside, before looking up at Flick. 'You don't need to look so shocked. I'm not suggesting some kind of macabre fashion show. I just thought…if you wore a dress for your next lesson, it might make a difference. You might understand what it is about dancing that's so…wonderful…'

'My next lesson?' It had been the last thing on Flick's mind today.

'You're not giving up already, are you? I'd thought better of you than that.'

'No, I'm not giving up.'

Yet. There had been an errant thought in

the back of her head, however, that her position here might not be tenable after what had happened last night. Oh…and there it was again…that rush of sensation that was her body announcing that it was properly coming back to life again. Like pins and needles in your foot after it had gone to sleep, only this was less painful and far more pleasurable.

'Choose a dress then. For next time. Not today because I'm too tired.'

It occurred to Flick that Lady Josephine might be asking for an assurance that she wasn't about to be abandoned so she complied with the odd request. It was easy to find a dress that she knew she'd love to try on. A ripple of silk in the darkest blue, with diamantés covering the bodice and scattered across acres of fabric that made up the ballerina-length skirt. She held it against her body, still in its plastic cover, and knew it would make her look more beautiful than she possibly ever had. It was a real Cinderella moment that reminded her of how she'd felt when she'd decided to stay in this remarkable old house—that she'd stepped into some kind of fairy tale and was up for the role of being a princess.

And...oh...after last night there was no one else who could be the prince other than Lachlan McKendry.

Flick had to close her eyes and take a very deep breath to try and centre herself before she took the dress back into the sitting room to show Lady Josephine, whose nod advertised satisfaction at her choice, if not approval.

'I won a national competition in that dress.'

'Shall I take it with me? I'd better try it on and make sure it fits before we have that lesson.'

The older woman shrugged. 'If you like. You can take the tray away, too.' She had turned to stare at the fire. 'Have you spoken to Lachlan today?'

'Um...no. Not since yesterday evening.'

The look she received didn't suggest disapproval or annoyance. Rather, it seemed like a request for information and Flick couldn't be anything less than honest.

'He's…upset. But…'

'But what?'

How much should she say? How much did Lady Josephine want to say? Flick could only follow her instincts here and they were personal rather than professional. She carefully draped the dress over the back of a chair and sat down on the edge of it herself.

'I don't think he was totally surprised to learn he was adopted,' she said quietly. 'He told me that he never really felt wanted.'

Flick could feel the ache of unshed tears. Last night, Lachlan's tears had captured her heart.

And there was no getting away from the fact that his lovemaking had captured her body and soul.

How could she keep working for the woman who was responsible for what had happened to make Lachlan feel that he'd had half his life stolen? Who had never felt loved?

'He wasn't my son.' Lady Josephine's words were fierce, as if she was being forced to admit something against her will. 'My sons died. All of them…'

Flick's indrawn breath was a gasp. '*All* of them?'

'Three. There were three.' Lady Josephine wasn't looking at Flick as she spoke. 'The first one, William, lived for three months and I loved him with all my heart.' She shook her head. 'As much as I adored my husband, even though I knew he was never faithful.'

She closed her eyes and stopped talking but Flick couldn't break the silence. She knew there was something more to be said and that it was important that she hear it. She listened to the rain now pelting the windows, instead, and just waited. She needed another piece of this puzzle. She even had the odd thought that she was meant to be here. To hear this. To be able to help people who needed more than her nursing skills?

'My second baby lived for a day,' Lady Josephine said finally, so quietly her voice was almost a whisper. 'The third was born dead, a month before he was due, but I didn't cry that time. I didn't even care any more...'

'It was too painful, wasn't it?' Flick suggested gently. 'Loving a baby and losing him is the kind of pain nobody feels they could ever bear to go through again.'

She knew that. Dear Lord, she knew that too well. She could almost feel the weight of an infant in her own arms who had never had the chance to take a breath. And maybe her knowledge of that pain came across as being as genuine as it was.

'I was glad—' Lady Josephine was watching her as she whispered '—that I didn't have to feel it again.'

'How long was it, after your last baby died, that you adopted Lachlan?'

Lady Josephine shrugged. 'I forget. A few weeks.' The breath she pulled in was wheezy. 'A couple of months, perhaps.' She had to take another breath after only a few words. 'It was Douglas who arranged everything...including the nannies.' She was reaching for her inhaler on the table. 'He made it easy for me to agree… Impossible not to.'

Flick got to her feet to help with the administration of the bronchodilator. Supporting Lady Josephine with her arm around the older woman's shoulders and her other hand holding the inhaler to press the top at just the right moment as a new breath was being taken felt like more than a simply professional touch.

It felt like a hug. An acknowledgement that her story had touched Flick on a very deep level even though she was so sympathetic to Lachlan's side of the same story. She could separate the strands to find herself alone but involved on both sides. Pulled in two directions, in fact, but it was easy to choose which one to focus on at this moment. She watched her patient carefully for signs that her respiratory distress was starting to ease but she decided another dose was necessary just a short time later.

'I'm going to give your doctor a call,' she said. 'That's two attacks in two days. You're under a lot of stress at the moment and it could be that you need something extra to help control things.'

Lady Josephine didn't put up an argument, which was an indication that her own life had been turned upside down as much as Lachlan's. The afternoon sped past with the doctor's visit, a new medical plan to be formulated and initiated, and new medications to be collected from the village pharmacy. It wasn't until much later that Flick had time to realise that perhaps Lachlan wasn't coming home tonight.

It was a shame, because she wanted a chance to tell him about that revealing conversation with his mother. It wasn't an excuse for the emotional damage done by the way he'd been raised. It might not lead to any kind of forgiveness, even, but it did provide a background that could at least offer a level of understanding. Flick was the right person to talk to him about it, as well, because she already understood.

She could imagine herself in Lady Josephine's position, with no escape from repeated grief that had left her too numb to be able to love that poor adopted baby. Fighting a depression that hadn't been recognised, let alone treated. Flick had been able to run from her grief and she'd kept running for years because it had been the perfect way to avoid loving anything enough for its loss to be painful. A job. A place. A person. Another baby would be unthinkable.

On the other hand, it might well be a good thing that Lachlan wasn't in the house tonight.

Because she was missing him too much already…?

It was when Flick was in the kitchen on an afternoon break the next day that she saw Lachlan again for the first time since their intimate night together.

Of course it was. This house might be the biggest Flick had ever lived in but most of her time with Lachlan had been in this one room. Talking time, anyway. Yesterday, she had been preoccupied with what silent messages might be communicated when they saw each other again but, now that it was happening, it was the last thing on Flick's mind. She was far more concerned about Lachlan's physical state.

'Are you okay? You look...'

'Wrecked. Yeah... I know.' Lachlan eyed the mug in front of Flick. 'Any more coffee in the pot?'

'You look like you need more than coffee.'

'You could be right. What's the best cure for a hangover?' Lachlan was rubbing his forehead in that gesture he'd told her he shared with his twin. 'I blame Josh,' he added. 'The whisky was his idea.' He sighed. 'I don't think I even had that much of it, mind you.'

'Headache?' Flick was taking in his pale skin and the circles under his eyes that looked dark enough to be bruises. 'I could find you some paracetamol. Have you had lunch yet?'

'I can't remember when I last ate. I was supposed to have dinner with Josh but he got the whisky out and we started talking and we didn't stop. We were up most of the night.'

So that was why he hadn't come home. Flick felt a wash of relief mix with her concern. He hadn't been somewhere else in order to avoid her. He'd been with his twin brother, taking the first steps in an astonishing and unexpected new relationship. And he'd now had two nights in a row with very little sleep? No wonder he was looking so wrecked.

'I could cook something,' she offered. 'Bacon and eggs are supposed to be good for a hangover.'

'I'm not that hungry.' Lachlan took a tumbler from a cupboard and filled it with water at the sink. 'Maybe I just need to catch up on some sleep. Or get a bit of fresh air.' He drank half the water. 'Besides, Tilly wouldn't be happy if we messed up her clean kitchen bench. Where is she?'

'Upstairs. Playing Scrabble with your mother while I take a bit of a break. It was rather a long day yesterday what with getting the doctor out again.'

But Lachlan wasn't about to enquire after his mother's health. In fact, Flick had seen the shutters come down as soon as she'd mentioned her. She could almost feel barriers being hastily erected. Lachlan drained his glass and set it down.

'Yep,' he said. 'Fresh air is the cure, I'm sure of it.'

His words were cheerful. He straightened up as he turned towards the door. He even found a smile and that reminded Flick of the persona she'd first met in this man. The one that could hide the real Lachlan McKendry so well. And it hurt, far more than she might have anticipated, to find herself being shut out like this.

She didn't want to be shut out. She needed to find a way to punch a hole in the barriers before they got any more solid.

'Thanks for the bluebells,' she found herself saying. 'They have the most amazing scent. It fills up my whole bedroom.'

Okay…that did it. Lachlan paused and turned. Maybe it was the mention of the bluebells or, more likely, the reference to a bedroom but the tension Flick had expected to be between them was definitely here. Strong enough to be using up all the oxygen in the room, in fact. For a long moment, they simply stared at each other and she could see just how torn Lachlan was.

He wanted to say something…but didn't want to at the same time.

He wanted to leave…but didn't want to…

The tension increased to a point where it had to break. Flick opened her mouth to say something but couldn't find any words. Maybe she was looking torn herself because something in Lachlan's expression softened.

'They smell even better in the woods,' he said quietly. 'Come and see…'

Flick was already on her feet but had barely been aware of moving. 'How far does the signal for the pager work?' she asked. 'In case I'm needed.'

'Far enough.' Lachlan was turning away again. 'But, in any case, Tilly can cope. She doesn't miss much so I expect she'll see where we're going from the window. You did say you're on a break?'

She had said that.

And it felt right to go with Lachlan, to

search in the boot room for a pair of wellies to cope with the damp ground after yesterday's rain and to follow him across a lawn now bathed in spring sunshine, because he had become an integral part of why she felt needed here.

Flick was tangled up in Lachlan's story as well as his mother's now and…and there were threads being woven into her own story that were too important to ignore. Whatever else was happening here, her own life was changing enough to make her feel she was standing at a very significant crossroads. Her body had not only come back to life thanks to Lachlan's touch, she was aware of a connection that was even more powerful. If she chose to, she could fall in love with this man and that opened possibilities that were so big they were terrifying.

She should be scared, she realised. She should probably choose a different path to go on at this unexpected crossroads but she didn't, because this, too, felt right. If he was inviting her, she needed to walk further on the same path as Lachlan. Until she could see where it might be leading, at least, and whether her heart had healed enough to be able to go there. If she needed to, she knew that she could turn around. She'd know the moment it didn't feel right and that would be the time to change direction completely and run. She could do that, too.

She'd had plenty of practice, after all.

CHAPTER EIGHT

SUNLIGHT FILTERED INTO the woods, making the new leaves on oak trees a soft, green halo above dark trunks and the carpet of blue flowers a stunning contrast.

The scent was strong enough to make Lachlan feel lightheaded for a moment. Or maybe his head was just so full of tumbling thoughts and emotions it was spinning out, giving up trying to find something solid and safe as an anchor.

It was Flick who reminded him that he was actually within the best anchor that he'd ever had—in a place he had always loved.

'This is *so* amazing. I'm scared to walk on them—I don't want to squash any flowers.'

'There are tracks. Like this one.'

Without thinking, Lachlan held out his hand to guide Flick onto one of the many paths that the deer followed in this forest. A sideways glance gave him another glimpse of Flick's delight and he realised that the bluebells darkened by this dappled light were an almost perfect match for the shade of blue of her eyes. A squirrel scurried up a trunk just ahead of them and Flick laughed, a joyous sound that—weirdly—brought the prickle of tears to the back of his eyes.

It was that sad/happy thing again. He probably should be letting go of Flick's hand by now but, instead, he found himself holding it a little tighter. And she didn't pull hers free.

'These are oak trees, yes?'

'Yes. They're the most common trees here but we also have chestnut and beech, ash and birch trees.'

'And squirrels. I love squirrels.'

'There are deer, as well. They keep these tracks open. I used to love seeing them. And hearing the woodpeckers or seeing owls.'

'This place is magic.' Flick's steps slowed as another swathe of bluebells appeared in front of them. 'I feel like I'm stepping into a fairy tale.' She was smiling up at him. 'And I think you were right.'

'About what?'

'Needing the fresh air. You're looking a bit better.'

He was feeling better, Lachlan realised. His head wasn't spinning any more. He was happy to be here. To be with Flick.

'This is home,' he told her quietly. 'When I think of my childhood home, it's not the house that comes to mind first. Or my parents. It's here, in these woods. Maybe it's the only part of my life that I feel I was lucky to have.'

That quirk of Flick's eyebrows was eloquent.

'Oh, I know how privileged I was to live like this and get the best education and opportunities. My life could have been so different. It could have easily been Josh here instead of me and I wouldn't have chosen his life.'

'Why not?'

'When we were talking last night, I got the impression that his whole life had been difficult. When he was just a little kid—about three—the people that adopted him had their own baby. A "real" son, Josh called him. He wasn't wanted any longer. By the time he was five, his parents were talking about putting him up for adoption again.'

Flick gasped. 'That's so awful.'

'His grandmother thought so, too, so she took him to live with her and it caused a family rift that was never fixed. Josh felt like it was his fault. That he was being cared for but he wasn't really wanted. Like me...'

Flick was still holding his hand and now she squeezed his fingers. 'It's an unbelievable coincidence,' she said. 'That you were both adopted and you both end up being doctors but even more, that you both had a childhood that nobody should have.' Her eyes were shining with potential tears. 'You should have been kept together. And had a family who loved you both.'

Lachlan's smile was wry. 'It's no wonder we found we have something else in common too.'

'What's that?'

'Neither of us has ever wanted to settle down. The idea of making a family of our own is the stuff of nightmares. He's the same as me with women—any hint of something permanent being wanted and we're running for the hills.'

Flick was smiling but her gaze slid away from his before he could read her expression. Her hand slid clear of his at the same time and she crouched quickly, as if she'd been waiting to touch the petals of the flowers at their feet, but Lachlan had the impression that she was deliberately creating distance between them.

He didn't like that. He wanted the closeness of the connection he'd discovered with this amazing woman. The closeness that meant he didn't have to hide anything about himself—even his tears. His night with Flick, on the day his world had imploded, felt like it had saved his life. Or at least his faith in humanity. He'd felt truly wanted for maybe the first time in his life. Truly cared for.

'I should head back,' Flick said as she

stood up. 'I've had more of a break than I usually do.' She was still smiling as she turned. 'Thank you so much for showing me the bluebells.'

Lachlan wanted to take her hand again and hold her here a little longer. Instead, he walked beside her and tried to close the gap in a different way.

'What is it that makes *you* run, Flick?'

Her glance was startled. 'What do you mean?'

'The way you live. Never staying long in one place. Never settling...'

'Been there, done that.' Her tone was dismissive. 'Didn't really work out that well.'

This time, Lachlan didn't resist the urge to take her hand. He pulled her to a stop.

'Tell me,' he said softly. And then, when he could see her hesitation, he held her gaze as well as her hand. 'Please... You know more about me than anyone else on the planet,' he added. 'But I don't know that much about you. Except that you can't dance very well.'

That made her smile. 'Hey... I'm getting lessons.'

He didn't want to even think about his mother, let alone ruin this moment by talking about her. He wanted to talk about Flick. To find out what was important to her. What she might consider to be home and whether it was about a place or a person. Perhaps she could see the questions in his eyes and how much he wanted the answers.

'I fell in love once.' She spoke slowly as she finally broke the silence. 'I married the man I loved—Patrick—and our life was perfect—right up until it all fell apart.'

Lachlan could see the depth of pain in her eyes.

'I lost our baby,' she said simply. 'Not that long before he was due to be born. And… that same week, Patrick got diagnosed with pancreatic cancer. I nursed him for a couple of months until he died and… I couldn't stay there any longer because it was too hard. I started moving and…and I guess I've never stopped. I've never wanted to stop because I might get caught by something. Or someone.' She dragged in a shaky breath. 'I could never survive loving and losing like that again.'

The woods around them were so quiet when Flick stopped speaking, Lachlan couldn't even hear a bird call. They were completely alone.

'We all have our stories,' Flick added softly. 'And real life is never a fairy tale so they don't always have happy endings, do they?'

Lachlan couldn't find any words to tell Flick how sorry he was that she'd suffered such tragedy. Or that if it were possible he'd want to erase at least some of that pain that kept her running. Telling her that, one day, she might find that she *could* turn the page and start a new chapter in her life would be dismissing an experience that had been so unbearable it was clearly going to leave shadows in her eyes for as long as she lived. But what he could do was to fold her into his arms and hold her. To try and give her the kind of comfort she had given him when he'd needed it most.

To let her know that he cared.

He had no idea how long they stood there in the warmth of the sunbeam that had found this spot, breathing in the delicate scent of the flowers around them, hearing faint birdsong and feeling each other's heartbeats. However long it was, it wasn't enough, though. And it was rudely broken by the strident sound of Flick's pager that carried a reminder of the real world and its hardships and, in particular, a person Lachlan still wasn't ready to even think about, let alone forgive.

'Good to know it works out here, I guess,' Flick said, as she pulled away from his arms. 'That means I can come out here again and smell the flowers when I need a break.'

'They'll be here for weeks,' Lachlan promised. 'There's plenty of time.'

Flick opened her mouth as if she was going to say something but then closed it again, giving her head a tiny shake to indicate that she'd changed her mind.

'You're right,' she murmured as she started walking again. 'There's plenty of time.'

* * *

She should have told him when she'd had the chance, days and days ago now.

Lachlan needed to know that there'd been a reason his adoptive mother couldn't love him—that it was about *her* and not him. And the perfect moment to have told him was after he'd been holding her and she could feel how much her own sad story had touched him.

But…*oh*…the way it had felt being held in his arms like that…

She hadn't let anyone that close since Patrick had died. Never. She'd never let anyone care about her that much because she wasn't prepared to take the risk of caring about *them* that much.

If she'd tried to talk about his mother right then, she would have seen those shutters come down again and he would have pushed her away because he was nowhere near ready to hear what she needed to tell him. And not only would it have ruined a memory of something so beautiful it could bring tears to her eyes—being held like that in a fairy tale, bluebell wood, it would have broken a new level of trust between them which was something that would be impossible to build again.

Like hope, trust was a fragile thing when it was newborn.

A precious thing.

Something that was getting stronger with every passing day but that only made it harder to risk testing it by pushing boundaries. Lachlan didn't want to speak to his mother. Or to see her. If he knew that she was watching from her windows when he came and went from the house, he gave no sign of it. Even now, as Lady Josephine waited for the few seconds it took for her blood glucose measurement to appear on the screen of the meter, her gaze was drifting towards the windows. She wanted to see Lachlan but she knew she had to wait for him to be ready, in the same way that Flick had known she had to wait for the right time to tell him what she knew about his mother.

Sometimes, the watching and waiting seemed like an exercise in frustration. Lach-

Ian commuted to London on more than one occasion and stayed overnight and when he was in residence he was leaving the house early and giving frequent evening lectures and training sessions that kept him out until late most nights.

Flick always waited up for him when she knew he was coming home because she knew she'd get that look. Sometimes it came after he'd had a meal that Mrs Tillman had left to keep warm in the oven or after he'd done some preparation for the next day's work but sometimes it came the moment his gaze met hers—especially if he'd been away for a day or two. It was the look that was an invitation to go to his room. Or hers. It didn't matter as long as it had a bed and a door they could use to close off the rest of the world. It had never been supposed to have been more than a one-off source of comfort on the night that Lachlan had been so upset but it had happened again, that evening after he'd taken Flick to see the bluebells and it had still felt like a source of comfort that night—maybe for both of them.

Over the last ten days, however, it had morphed into something rather different. Something that still held an element of comfort for people whose life experiences had led them to choose to face life alone but there were definitely new levels of physical pleasure being woven into their private time together and it was the kind of pleasure that could rapidly become addictive.

Flick would find herself holding her breath as she waited for that look and it was more need than desire that was stealing her ability to draw in more air. She was desperate for an invitation that was only becoming more and more irresistible as they got to know each other's bodies more and more intimately. How could it take no more than a glance to ignite a passion that could not only last for hours but get more intense every time?

She knew perfectly well that she was breaking rules. That having a sexual relationship with her employer was completely unprofessional but…she was hooked and it seemed like Lachlan was equally caught and it was just as unprofessional from his side of the equation, wasn't it? It was a shared guilt but there was also an unspoken but shared excuse that made it less of an issue. Lachlan had made it very clear that his relationships were only ever short-lived and he knew it was the same for Flick. That they would only have a short time together because he would head back to his London life soon enough and she would move on to another locum position.

Given the effort that Lady Josephine was putting into her own care since the shock of the confrontation with Lachlan, it seemed quite likely that a full-time carer would not be needed in this house for much longer. Lady Josephine's confession about her past had changed something that made Flick wonder if that had been the first time she had ever spoken about the grief of losing her own babies and feeling unable to love her adopted son.

The shock of recognising how much damage had been done could have made the older woman withdraw even more into herself but, somehow, the opposite seemed to be happening. Was Lachlan's mother trying to find a way to make an apology? Or, at the very least, not be a burden?

Whatever it was, it was making a big difference. Lady Josephine was taking control of her own medications and monitoring, like performing her own finger prick tests to measure her level of blood glucose. Her use of the preventative medication for her asthma had meant she hadn't had another attack and she was exercising more and more. She was giving Flick dancing lessons in the ballroom almost every day. She was walking in the gardens and had even ventured into the woodland yesterday. There was a tiny vase on her table right now that had a few bluebells in it.

Flick would never see or smell these flowers again without being able to feel what it had been like to be in Lachlan's arms. As Lady Josephine recorded her BGL in her medical diary, Flick found herself reaching for the vase, so that she could pick it up and hold it close to her nose and soak in that gorgeous scent and it was at that moment that she realised she'd been very wrong about something. Two things, in fact.

She'd thought she'd know when it was time to run.

She'd thought she had a choice about whether or not she was going to fall in love with Lachlan McKendry.

But the rush of emotion as she breathed in the scent of being held in Lachlan's arms told her just how wrong she'd been. This wasn't just the scent of new beginnings for her. It was the scent of being cared for.

Being loved...

And returning love...

She knew, at that instant, that she was way past the point of no return on both her assumptions and she had no idea what she was going to do about it. She couldn't simply run and leave her patient before she knew she could look after herself. And she couldn't fall out of love, could she?

Perhaps Lady Josephine noticed the slight tremble in her fingers as she carefully put the vase down again.

'Lachlan used to bring me big bunches of bluebells when he was a little boy.'

'He told me that.' Flick met her gaze. She didn't say anything about how it had made Lachlan feel when his offerings had been rejected but there was a new level of trust between the two women and a growing ability to communicate by saying very little.

'I couldn't bear it,' the older woman added softly. 'They smelt like tears...'

Flick's heart was breaking for her. She had wanted to love her adopted son but she'd been pushed past the point of endurance and forced to find a safe place.

She was in desperate need of at least understanding, if forgiveness wasn't possible.

Flick had to hope the right moment to talk to Lachlan about this would present itself soon—in a way that would mean he wouldn't push her away and slam the door. With the disturbing revelation of how deeply she was now involved—how deeply she was in love with Lachlan—the prospect of breaking that connection had just become a whole lot bigger. So huge, Flick felt a trickle of fear shimmy down her spine.

'He needs time,' she said aloud. 'I know how hard it is but... I think everybody needs more time to get their heads around it all.'

Including herself.

CHAPTER NINE

TONIGHT WAS ONE of the nights Lachlan had
something to do to prepare for a training
session at Gloucester General Hospital the
next day.

'Has Tilly gone home already?'

'Yes…why? Are you hungry?'

'No. I ate in town. I had an appointment
with a butcher. I don't think Tilly would be
happy to have this in the fridge overnight so
it's good that she's gone home.' He put down
the two, large cool boxes. 'Want to see?'

'Sure.'

'It's for a workshop that's lined up for tomorrow. Advanced suturing. In particular,
running subcuticular sutures.' Lachlan only
met Flick's gaze briefly as he lifted out a
small section of pig skin from the bags he
was fitting into the fridge. He knew if he

caught that gaze for too long, he'd forget all about anything he needed to do this evening because the only thing that would be filling his mind would be how soon he could get Flick alone—in his bedroom.

What had started unexpectedly in the confusion of his world being upended had changed into something that he just couldn't get enough of. He couldn't call it 'Fun' exactly, because that was far too pale a word to come anywhere near describing what it was like to make love with Flick. It was the best thing that had ever happened to him and it had come when he'd needed it the most. A lifeline that he wasn't ready to let go of just yet. But, right now, it would have to wait and this was a good test to see if he could ignore the temptation.

Flick was peering at the skin. 'What's happened to it?'

'We gave it a nice, jagged laceration. The butcher found a metal tool that was perfect for the job and he was only too happy to help me prepare the samples. I've got some with nice, neat surgical incisions but what I really want to teach in the workshop is how you can make a wound as messy as this into a candidate for the suture technique that gives the best possible cosmetic result. I just need to check that it's going to work.' He opened his satchel to take out a suture kit.

Lachlan could feel Flick watching him as he set up a board to use on the kitchen table and he knew she was genuinely interested in what he was telling her. He liked that. He also liked the feeling of control he had right now because it gave him confidence that the strength of his desire for Flick wasn't going to end up being a problem. He'd be able to walk away when he needed to, just as he had done with every relationship he'd ever had with a woman.

'So, some people argue that tissue adhesive gives just as good, if not a better result but there are times when glue isn't going to be enough to hold things together and this is a great technique to have up your sleeve.'

He picked up a needle with its attached thread. 'The secret is to decontaminate a wound very thoroughly and then make the edges straight.'

Flick was sitting on the edge of the chair beside him, leaning in to watch what he was doing. 'How do you do that? There are no straight edges at all.'

'Like this… I'm using a whip stitch and taking the smallest possible bites to bring the edges together.' Years of perfecting his skills enabled him to work swiftly and precisely. 'Then I'm going to use the scalpel and run it down one side of the line of stitching and then the other and…*voila*…' he lifted the thin, jagged segment of skin clear, leaving two straight clean edges.

'Okay, I'm impressed.'

'But wait…' Lachlan grinned at her. 'There's more.'

With a new suture, he anchored a stitch at one end of the laceration and then took tiny bites parallel to the wound, just under the surface of the skin. When he got to the other end, he anchored another knot into the deeper, dermal layer and buried it under the skin by taking the needle out a little way away from the end of the cut. When he snipped the thread, it retracted under the skin and all the suture material was completely invisible and the edges of the laceration were in perfect alignment.

'That would barely leave a scar at all in real skin, would it?'

'That's the plan. Doesn't work if there's too much tension, of course. Or on thin skin like an eyelid but it has its place. I've got a good group coming tomorrow. GPs, surgeons and ED staff. Some nurses doing advanced training as well.'

'I started my nursing career in Emergency.' Flick sounded thoughtful. 'Maybe I should see if I can get my next locum gig in an ED. I miss this kind of stuff.'

'Why not a permanent job instead of a locum? That way, you could get to do some advanced training, maybe, and go to cool workshops like mine.'

He couldn't read her expression but it reminded him of when she'd stopped herself saying something that day he'd taken her to see the bluebells. As if she'd thought better of whatever it was she'd intended to say.

Was she wondering whether she might actually prefer to settle somewhere for a while? To stop running? It would be a good thing if she was because she deserved to start that new chapter in her life. One that might even make up for the sadness she'd had to live with.

There was certainly a hint of wariness in those gorgeous, blue eyes and her lips were parted, ready to speak. Or to kiss… This time, Lachlan caught her gaze and kept holding it until he saw that wariness replaced by desire as her eyes darkened and the tip of her tongue came out to touch her lips. In slow motion, perhaps because they were both savouring every heartbeat of the anticipation, they leaned closer. Until their lips were touching. Until the kiss stole any remnants of that control Lachlan had thought he'd had.

But it didn't matter.

He knew it would be there when he needed it again and he didn't need it yet.

Who wouldn't want to make the most of this while it lasted and who knew how long that might be?

The skills Lachlan had demonstrated when he'd been showing Flick the suture technique he intended teaching had been impressive.

The skills he demonstrated in her bed a short time later were even more impressive. Or maybe it didn't take that much skill when even the lightest touch of his hands on her body was enough to take Flick to a place where nothing else mattered. Where passion could explode with such power but so gently it was heart-breaking.

This wasn't the first time that Flick had felt a tear trickling down the side of her nose as she lay in Lachlan's arms as their breathing and heart rates slowly returned to normal and they came back to the real world, but it was the first time that she understood why this was so poignant.

It was because she was in love with Lachlan.

Because—even though she had told him

she could never risk this kind of love when it came with the potential of devastating loss—it had happened anyway.

And she wanted this feeling for ever.

The feeling that she knew she could only ever have if she was in this man's arms.

And she knew it couldn't be for ever because he'd spelt it out, that day in the blue-bell wood.

He's the same as me with women—any hint of something permanent being wanted and we're running for the hills...

The day that she should have told him what she knew about his mother. Flick's heart rate picked up again as she summoned enough courage to do what she should have done then.

'You asleep?' she asked softly.

'Not yet.' Lachlan's arms tightened around Flick. 'I should be. Can't believe how tiring this training programme is proving to be.'

'It's not as if it's the only thing you've got going on in your life. I'm not surprised it's hard work.'

'I feel like I'm pushing something very

heavy uphill half the time. Life's just got too complicated. Too different.' With her cheek against Lachlan's chest, she could feel that his heart missed a beat. 'I've got a brother now. Real family and that's making me have to think about the future and that's not something I've ever done. Not in personal terms, anyway. Career, yes. Family, no. Because I didn't think I had a family.'

'But you do...' Flick's thoughts were threatening to run in a different direction. If Lachlan was starting to think about a future that included family, could that mean he might consider changing his stance when it came to relationships with women? With *her*?

'I had a meeting with Josh today. I'm doing a nerve transplant surgery on one of his patients—a two-year-old boy called Toby who's lost effective use of one arm after breaking his collarbone and doing some significant damage to the brachial plexus network of nerves. And—' Flick could hear a smile in his voice '—he reminded me that I'd suggested we have a night out for dinner, including his friend Stevie, some time. As a kind of "thank you" for the way she saved us from having to meet for the first time in front of a whole bunch of people.

'I've been wanting to take you out some-where nice because you deserve a proper night off,' he added. 'So how 'bout it? Din-ner at one of the best restaurants the Cots-wolds has to offer?'

'Sounds fabulous,' Flick said. 'And… speaking of dinner, I need to tell you that your mother's decided to stop eating dinner in her room. She's going to come down and start using the dining room again. I think she's really hoping that you might join her one night.'

The silence from Lachlan was a warn-ing that he didn't want to talk about this but Flick had to ignore it.

'There's something else I have to tell you. That I should have told you as soon as I knew but I was worried that you might think I was interfering or that it might be too much on top of everything else and you'd just leave. I… I didn't want you to leave…'

Oh, man…that was almost a confession that she was in love with him, wasn't it? She could feel how still Lachlan was and the odd tension in his muscles that was holding him like that.

'I told you that I lost my baby,' Flick said quietly. 'So I know how hard it was that your mother lost a baby. Not just one baby. Three of them. Three boys, one after the other. I think it must have been something genetic that caused it. She had her heart completely broken by the first death of the baby she'd loved and nurtured for three months. By the time she had a very late miscarriage—like mine—with her third baby, she was past being able to grieve. And that was when your father arranged for your adoption. Can you imagine what it was like for her to be expected to become a loving mother to a child who wasn't her own—and at a time when she must have felt that life wasn't even worth living?'

Lachlan slipping his arm from beneath Flick's head as he sat up in her bed felt like her worst fears were about to come true. He was going to push her away and simply walk out. She bit her lip as she heard him blow out a stunned breath.

'Wow...' Lachlan was silent for a long moment as he tried to gather his thoughts. 'I never knew.' There was a fight going on in his head now. Or was it his heart? He could feel the yearning he'd had to be loved as a small boy and the pain of never feeling good enough battling with his empathy for someone who'd been through such a devastating experience.

'I feel sorry for her, of course,' he added, 'but I can't promise it's going to change how I feel about her. Or how I remember my childhood.' He shook his head. 'It's another thing I have in common with Josh in a way, isn't it? His adopted family had their "real" son after he was adopted. Mine had them before but the result's been remarkably similar, hasn't it? Two people who don't trust in family or want to risk trying to make their own.'

He didn't want to think about it any longer because this was yet another revelation that was shaking the foundations of his life. Lachlan needed a distraction. Fast.

'What's that?' he asked. 'Hanging on the back of your door?'

He hadn't noticed it when he'd pushed the door shut behind them. Why would he have when all he'd been able to think about had been Flick and what they were about to do. Every time, he wondered whether their love-making could possibly be as good as the last time and he was always astonished that it could actually be better. He knew exactly what kind of touch would elicit those delicious sounds of a need that matched his own and how to keep Flick teetering on the brink of paradise until she begged for release. Tonight, he'd even managed to time it so that they fell over the edge together, which was yet another new and amazing experience for Lachlan.

'It's a ball gown,' Flick told him. 'I haven't worn it yet, because I decided I needed to know how to dance a lot better first, but I got it out because I thought I might be able to wear it for my lesson tomorrow.'

Oh…this was the perfect distraction even if he was so tired it felt like he needed to sleep for a week. Lachlan didn't want to go back to his own room yet, though. He didn't want to be alone with his thoughts.

'Wear it now,' he said softly, bending down to kiss Flick's lips.

He saw her tongue come out to lick her bottom lip—as if she wanted to taste him again—and that created a flash of pleasure that was sharp enough to puncture the cloud of confused thoughts vying for time in his head.

His smile was intended to persuade her. 'Wear it for me,' he whispered.

He watched her getting out of the bed, taking the dress from its plastic package and stepping into it. He got up himself, so that he could pull the zip up at the back. Knowing that she had no underwear on beneath those slippery ripples of fabric was arousing him all over again. This was certainly the best distraction ever.

'It fits,' Flick murmured. 'Your mother was right when she said I was the same size she used to be when she danced in competitions. She won something big wearing this dress.'

Okay…more distraction was needed. Lachlan hurriedly pulled on his jeans. He put his shirt on but couldn't waste time doing up any buttons.

'Come with me.' He took hold of Flick's hand without allowing her any time to protest but she didn't seem to mind. Both barefoot, they tiptoed along the hallway that went past his mother's bedroom and then raced silently down the stairs. When they reached the ballroom, Lachlan put on only as many of the small, side lights as it took to lift the darkness to a point where he could see the shimmer of the sparkles in Flick's dress and he put his phone in his pocket, so that only they would be able to hear the soft music.

And then they danced. Barefoot. Flick's hair was a tumble of classic 'bed hair' ruffled waves and he couldn't forget that she was naked beneath a dress that was even more gorgeously sparkly in this soft light. Lachlan was half-naked himself with his shirt unbuttoned and the sleeves rolled up. He was tired enough for this to feel as if it was part of a dream. Maybe that was why Flick felt so light in his arms and how she responded to his lead as if she'd been dancing her whole life.

They circled the parquet floor once and then again. There was no stepping on toes but, rather, a feeling of connection that was almost a continuation of their lovemaking.

It felt like flying.

It felt like falling at the same time.

Falling in love…?

The music ended almost as he had that thought and Lachlan could only stare at Flick, stunned by what had just hit him completely unexpectedly.

He saw the lines of concern appear on her face. 'You look *so* tired,' she whispered. 'You need to sleep.'

He did. Maybe, by some miracle, things would look different in the morning. He would have come back to his senses. But he couldn't go upstairs to his own room without saying something.

'You've learned to dance.' His words were soft. 'You are an amazing woman, Felicity Stephens. I hope you know that.'

There was a smile on her lips as she stood on tiptoe to place a soft kiss on his.

'I think it was the dress that made the difference. Only I need to take it off. This bodice is tight enough to be really uncomfortable.'

Lachlan couldn't help letting his gaze drop to the swell of her breasts over that beaded bodice but it only made him want Flick all over again. Made him want to somehow keep what they had for ever.

He swallowed hard. This was the kind of dangerous territory he'd always kept very well clear of.

'Goodnight, Flick,' he murmured. 'Sleep well.'

CHAPTER TEN

'I THINK WE'RE good to go.' Lachlan tapped the paper in front of him. 'I'm happy with these results of the repeat nerve function electrical test. It sets us up to use the classic approach to repairing the brachial plexus network.'

Josh looked up from the detailed result sheets they'd both been studying. 'That's where you use the distal branches of the spinal accessory nerve to neurotise the suprascapular nerve?'

'It is. I'll find the donor nerve first because that's easier than locating the suprascapular notch and nerve.'

'I'm looking forward to watching. You're not bothered that the gallery's going to be packed?'

'I'm getting used to things like that. I've

been in London today, filming a follow-up appointment with a boy that's part of a medical documentary. I did a masseteric nerve transfer surgery to treat his facial paralysis a few weeks ago. It'll take months to get the full benefit but he's putting everything he has into retraining his muscles. We're just beginning to see the first signs and he's so excited. It's the kind of thing I love most about my job.'

'It can't be easy flitting back and forth like that and then having a late night like this. No wonder you look done in.'

'Yeah.' Lachlan rubbed the back of his neck. 'I think I'll just crash in town tonight.'

'Come home with me?'

'Thanks, but I rather fancy a nice hotel with room service. Close enough to walk in and get some fresh air before the surgery tomorrow. I'm not getting enough exercise at the moment. My joints are making me feeling twice as old as I am.'

'As *we* are.' Josh smiled. 'I feel like that sometimes. I'm getting older way too fast.' His smile faded. 'Are things no better with your mother, then? Is that part of why you don't want to go home tonight?'

Lachlan shrugged. 'Maybe. I'm still trying to get my head around it all, you know?'

He didn't want to share the new information he had about Josephine McKendry with Josh yet. Not until he was sure about how he felt about it and he was too exhausted to go there right now. Or to think about how he was feeling about Flick, for that matter. He owed it to his small patient to be in the best possible form tomorrow morning and that meant pushing anything personal aside.

'There's a great hotel just a block or so away. I'll walk out with you and point you in the right direction.'

'Thanks, mate.'

A cleaner who was mopping the floor outside the ground floor pharmacy did a double-take of the two identical men walking past him but neither Lachlan nor Josh were bothered. They were getting used to it, now. Getting used to the idea of being related, too.

Family.

One of the 'F' words that Lachlan had long

considered against the rules, along with 'Full time' and 'Future'. The opposite of the acceptable 'Fun'.

Good Lord…had he really been that shallow such a short time ago?

He paused as the brothers stood outside the hospital but he wasn't taking any notice of the direction Josh was pointing in.

'Do you think it made it easier?' he asked, 'Knowing all along that you'd been adopted?'

'I think it made it worse,' Josh told him. 'I knew I was different. That I didn't belong, somehow, but I didn't know why until a "real" son came along and I wasn't wanted any more.'

Lachlan shook his head. 'I never knew and I think that was worse because I didn't belong either but I never knew why. Until I met you.'

And the truth had finally come out. How much worse would it have been if Flick hadn't been there at the start of all this? How much harder would it be when she'd moved on, possibly in the not so distant future? At least Lachlan could be thankful that he hadn't said anything about how he was feeling about her in the ballroom last night. If he had, she might have packed her bags already. She'd made it very clear why she lived a nomadic kind of life.

'I've never wanted to stop because I might get caught by something. Or someone...'

'I could never survive loving and losing like that again...'

'Real life is never a fairy tale...'

Josh's glance suggested he could guess that Lachlan's thoughts were straying. 'Life's got a bit crazy, hasn't it? For both of us.'

'You're not wrong there. I've got too many things changing too fast and I've never liked feeling that I'm not in control.' Lachlan let his breath out in a sigh. 'Ah, well...tomorrow's another day, huh? Show me again where the hotel is?'

Being taken out by Lachlan to have dinner with his brother and friend at one of the most prestigious, Michelin-starred restaurants in the area felt very much like they were on a double date. As if their secret, temporary relationship had just been elevated to a new level. Nothing with any promise of permanence, of course, but the way Lachlan's hands shaped Flick's shoulders as he helped her to shrug off her coat made her realise just how comfortable they were as a couple now. How easy it was to communicate with simply a touch or a glance.

Which was why Lachlan probably knew how startled she was to find herself with another version of him. For a while, she felt as awkward as Lachlan had clearly been the night before, when he'd finally agreed to join his mother for dinner in what seemed to be a first, tentative step on both their parts to move forward. Not that they'd discussed anything personal but Flick, who'd also been invited to join them, had felt like the polite conversation was a cautious attempt to find common ground that could be built on later.

Being introduced to Josh and his friend Stevie as 'Felicity' made things even more awkward.

'Call me Flick,' she'd told them. 'I've only

ever been called Felicity by the taxman or the police.'

'What were the police after you for?' Lachlan was smiling as he caught her gaze. 'No, don't tell me… I think I'd rather leave that to my imagination for a while.'

Oh…that smile. That rather intimate innuendo that came with his words made it seem like they'd been doing this for ever. Dating. Being out in public as a real couple.

And it felt so right that Flick found herself relaxing as drinks were ordered and menus perused. It didn't surprise her at all that both she and Lachlan chose the same starter of hay-smoked scallops.

'How's that lad doing?' Lachlan asked Josh. 'From the brachial plexus repair?'

'Very well…'

'I've been trying to get back to see him again but it's been full on.' Lachlan put down his fork although he'd barely tasted his food. 'Lectures here, surgeries there and I've had to dash up to London a couple of times as well.'

'Sounds stressful.' Josh sounded sympathetic.

'At least I don't have to worry about anything on the home front.' He raised his glass in Flick's direction. 'You're doing a fabulous job,' he told her. 'I'm not at all surprised that London Locums considers you to be one of their very best nurses. I will be grateful to you for ever. For everything…'

Flick had to break that eye contact—before Lachlan could see just how much his praise and appreciation was melting her. How much she loved him… She stared at her plate, even closing her eyes for a heartbeat to try and regain control.

Josh's question about how long she'd been a locum nurse was a welcome direction to take her thoughts.

'Oh, years…' Flick found a smile for Lachlan's brother. 'I love the excitement of everything being new. Meeting new people, getting to know a new place. A new challenge…'

She stopped talking, her gaze shifting instantly to Lachlan as he made an odd sound of discomfort.

'It's a bit warm in here, isn't it?' Flick watched, concerned, as he rubbed his forehead in a familiar gesture that indicated stress. Then he pushed back his chair. 'Excuse me for a moment. I just need a bit of fresh air.'

Concern became a flash of alarm as Flick watched Lachlan head for a set of French doors near their table that led to a pretty courtyard garden with manicured hedges and strings of fairy lights. She pushed her plate away and had her hands on the table ready to push herself to her feet and go after Lachlan but Josh had moved first.

'I'll go,' he said.

She was still watching as Josh joined his brother outside and started talking to him. This was good. Josh was a doctor and, if Lachlan was unwell in any way, he would be able to help better than Flick could. What was really worrying her, however, was the level of her concern.

She knew she had fallen in love with Lachlan McKendry. She hadn't quite realised until now just how profound her feelings were, though, had she? This wasn't just concern that someone she cared about might be unwell. This was a twinge of a fear that she'd had to face before—that the person she couldn't live without might be in danger...

Oh, boy...she might be in a bit of trouble here.

Catching a glance from Stevie only strengthened the instant connection she'd felt for this friend of Lachlan's brother with her gorgeously wild, red hair and big, genuine smile.

She wasn't the only one who was in love with a twin, was she?

Not that either of them wanted to say anything aloud. There was a note in that glance that was one of understanding. They both knew how the childhoods of these twins who'd been separated had shaped a remarkably similar attitude to whether they wanted a permanent relationship in their own lives. Flick could recognise things in Stevie's eyes that she was feeling herself. Like hope. And fear.

It was that fear that made her look outside again and then it suddenly became infinitely worse because she saw the moment when Lachlan became unsteady on his feet and then crumpled, clearly having lost consciousness. Josh caught his brother in time to stop him hitting his head on the flagstone terrace and Flick could see him crouching to see if Lachlan was breathing by the time she'd run from the table and pushed open the French doors, Stevie on her heels.

'What can I do?' It was Stevie who spoke first as they got to the two men.

Flick's brain was frozen. With her experience in emergency departments, she should know exactly what to do but the fear was paralysing her now.

'Oh, my God…' she whispered, dropping to her knees beside Lachlan. She could actually feel the blood draining from her face. *'No…'*

She touched Lachlan's hand. Curled her own fingers around it and held it tightly, as if she could somehow share some of her own strength. Above her, Josh's words seemed faint—as if they were coming from a long way away.

'He's breathing. And he's got a good, steady pulse. He may have just fainted for whatever reason but I think we'd better call an ambulance.'

Flick was still clinging to Lachlan's hand as he regained consciousness before help arrived but he still seemed drowsy and his speech was slurred enough for the paramedics to be concerned. They helped him into the back of the ambulance to take an ECG and check vital signs like his blood pressure, blood glucose level and oxygen saturation. One of them asked how much alcohol he'd had but Josh was insistent that there was something more going on here and that scared Flick even more.

What was going on and how serious could it be?

Lachlan had picked up on a note in his brother's voice and he was trying to sit up. 'Gotta go home...' he said. 'It's my mother... she's the one who's sick...'

'She's all right,' Flick reassured him. 'I just

rang Mrs Tillman to tell her that I would be going to the hospital with you so I might be later than expected.'

But Lachlan was shaking his head. 'No need. I'm fine. And it's my mother you're employed to care for...not *me*... I don't need it... Can look after myself...'

He was pushing her away. Like she had feared he might when she'd been avoiding telling him what she'd learned about his mother's story. She knew how badly she didn't want to be pushed out of his life. How much it could hurt. But she'd had no idea, had she? This was hurting far more than Flick had ever imagined it could.

Especially now. When Lachlan was sick. Possibly afraid. When he most needed someone who cared to be by his side. And that person should be her but then Josh spoke.

'I'll go with Lachlan,' he said.

His gaze told her that he understood. That she wasn't to worry because he wasn't about to leave his brother alone even if Lachlan was so sure he could cope without anybody. And Josh had more right to be with Lachlan at a time like this, didn't he? He was family. Not just someone who'd been employed to care for his mother. Lachlan had said he didn't need her.

Perhaps he didn't want her, either...

CHAPTER ELEVEN

THERE'D BEEN A few things in Lachlan Mc-Kendry's thirty-six years on earth that had scared him enough to be memorable but this particular moment made every other occasion instantly insignificant.

'I'm sorry to have to give you this result, but it's AML.' David, the consultant and head of the haematology department, clearly knew he didn't have to elaborate on the diagnosis to the two other doctors in the room but perhaps he didn't realise that the third person present had medical knowledge. 'Acute myeloid leukaemia,' he added quietly, his gaze shifting to Flick.

Lachlan closed his eyes as he shifted in the bed, trying to find a more comfortable position. The local anaesthetic in his hip had worn off some time ago and a dull ache was making sure he didn't forget the bone marrow biopsy he'd had first thing this morning. Or why it had been necessary.

He heard Josh clear his throat. 'We kind of guessed it might be, last night,' he told David. 'When we added up his symptoms after that first blood count had come through.' He was standing close to the bed. 'But I was still hoping we could be wrong.'

Lachlan could see a reflection of his own fear in Josh's eyes and he didn't want that, any more than he'd wanted his brother to stay with him after that first, worrying test result last night. He wasn't used to having someone who genuinely cared about what was happening to him because he'd never let anyone that close and…it made things harder. You had to worry about them, as well as yourself.

'A normal level of blasts—the immature white blood cells—should be less than five percent,' David said, breaking the sombre silence in the room. 'Yours are over twenty percent, Lachlan.'

Lachlan didn't want to look at Flick to see

how she was taking the news. Because he was afraid she would look like Josh did? Or more afraid that she wouldn't—that she was only here out of politeness or perhaps, at best, friendship?

'Is there a genetic component?' he asked. 'Because, if there is, maybe Josh is at risk and he'd better get himself tested as well.'

'I did read about a case of identical twins getting diagnosed with AML a few days apart,' Josh said. 'Probably because I was up half the night, reading.' He offered Lachlan an apologetic smile. 'Concordant AML, it's called, but the good news is that they had a sibling who was an HLA match and they got a stem cell transplant, which has apparently cured them. They didn't even get any graft versus host disease.'

HLA. Human leukocyte antigens? Lachlan needed to do a bit of reading himself and refresh everything he knew about haematology.

'A bone marrow/stem cell transplant, with or without chemotherapy, certainly offers the potential of a complete cure,' David nodded. 'But we're a wee way away from talking about that yet. What we need to focus on right now is some more tests to collect as much information as we can about the subtype and staging and then we'll be able to plan your chemotherapy regime, Lachlan. I'd like to start as soon as possible. Tomorrow, even.'

So, there it was.

This was real. And urgent. This wasn't just yet another revelation to add to the ones that had turned Lachlan's life inside out in recent weeks. They had merely been warning shots and now his life was actually imploding. Josh clearly wanted to believe he was going to have a positive outcome like the case he'd read about but there was also a distinct possibility that he was facing the end of his life.

And it was scaring the hell out of him.

And...he couldn't help looking at Flick now. He wanted nothing more than to be alone with her. For her to put her arms around him and hold him so tightly he could think about nothing more than how much he needed her.

How much he loved her... If he'd had any doubts at all about how he felt about this woman, the thought that he might not live much longer had just wiped them out completely. It was strange how it could focus the mind like a laser beam on what was actually important in life.

And that was people.

Love.

He'd learned to live without it. Avoid it. How ironic was it that he'd found two people who represented the best of what people and love could offer, just in the last few weeks? Which meant this was going to affect them as well.

Hurt them.

Neither of them deserved that but it was especially awful for Flick when she'd been through this before. If he'd been unsure of whether he would see how much she cared when he caught her gaze, those doubts had also evaporated completely. She looked easily as pale and sick as he was feeling himself. As if she was already hurting past the point of it being bearable—because she really did care about him.

Loved him, even—as much as he loved her?

He couldn't do this to her. Or to Josh. He could sense how much his brother wanted to be involved—how connected he was—but maybe the only way Lachlan could show how much *he* cared was to spare him the kind of pain that could well be on the way. The kind they all knew about, that came with either losing or not receiving the love they needed so much.

Lachlan deliberately shuttered his gaze as he held eye contact with Flick. An unspoken denial of how he felt about her. A non-verbal shove that was intended to tell her the opposite, in fact. That he didn't need her. Or want her.

And the message seemed to have got through because Flick appeared to shrink back. To gather herself in some way that made her seem smaller and more vulnerable.

Her voice sounded different, too. As though it was someone else that was speaking.

'I'm so sorry,' she said. 'But I can't do this again...'

Lachlan had already broken the eye contact but he could see her in his peripheral vision. And he could see the shock on Josh's face when she turned and walked out of the room.

He didn't feel shocked.

He felt...relieved... Surely it would be far better for her in the long run to be angry with him and get as far away as possible. He couldn't blame her for running. He'd do it himself, if he could.

History was not supposed to repeat itself. Not this kind of history, anyway, and especially not when you'd done everything possible to make absolutely sure it *couldn't* repeat itself.

Flick actually felt so physically sick she went into the nearest toilets and ran cold water to cup in her hands and splash onto her face.

Leukaemia.

Cancer.

Watching someone that you loved *this* much slip away from you and being unable to help. Having your heart break, again and again, into tiny shards that she now knew could make you bleed inside for years and years.

She couldn't do this again because she wouldn't survive.

Even now, as Flick left the shelter of the bathroom and made her way to the front door of Cheltenham Central Hospital, she could feel the cracks widening in her heart already and the pain was enough to make her feel unsteady on her feet. She stopped again, beside a kiosk in the main entrance that sold magazines and newspapers.

'Are you all right, love?' The woman in the kiosk was leaning over the counter to peer at Flick.

'I'm...fine...'

Flick reached out towards a tall, rotating stand of magazines in the hope that it would provide support. But even as she touched it, she could feel it falling away and taking her with it.

And then everything went dark.

'Ah...there you are. Welcome back.'

'Where am I?'

'In the emergency department of Cheltenham Central. You passed out in our foyer and someone carried you in here a few minutes ago. What's your name?'

'Flick...'

'Pardon?' The young doctor was looking bemused.

'Officially, it's Felicity. Felicity Stephens.' The lights above her were very bright so Flick screwed up her eyes. Was that why she could suddenly see Lachlan in her mind? And hear his voice as he used her proper name?

'I'm so sorry, Felicity... I've had a rather difficult day and I suspect you might very well be the answer to my prayers.'

More than that. She could see that first glimpse of who Lachlan McKendry really was under that polished and sophisticated exterior. The real man who was upstairs in this hospital and…and she couldn't afford to start thinking about him. Not if she was going to survive.

'But you prefer to be called Flick?' The junior ED medic was on top of things now. 'How old are you, Flick? And do you have any underlying medical conditions I should know about?'

'I'm thirty-two. And, no… I'm perfectly healthy. I'm just a bit stressed, that's all. And I skipped breakfast.'

'As a rule, perfectly healthy people don't faint and remain unconscious for a while. We'd like to run a few tests before we let you go, okay?'

'I need to get home. I'm a nurse. I have someone to look after.' Flick tried to sit up only to find her head was still spinning a little. And she didn't need to rush back to Lady Josephine. In fact, she'd been ordered not to.

I can look after myself, for heaven's sake. I should have been doing it years ago. Go and find what's happening with my…with

Lachlan. Please... I need to know he's all right.'

'As a nurse, you'll know we have a protocol to try and identify the cause of unconsciousness.' The doctor was wrapping a tourniquet around her arm. 'We'll take some bloods, do a finger prick for your BGL and do an ECG. Any chance you could be pregnant?'

A huff of something like laughter came from Flick's throat. That would be the straw that broke the camel's back, wouldn't it?

'No chance,' she said. But there was a tiny voice at the back of her head, reminding her of that first time she and Lachlan had made love. When emotions had been running so high that night in the wake of Lachlan learning not only that he'd been adopted but that his mother had never wanted him, protection hadn't crossed their minds. But it had only been the once and...and how long ago *had* that been?

The doctor must have seen the flash of alarm in her eyes.

'We'll do a urine dipstick as well, just to

cover all the bases. It'll be quicker than the blood test.'

Quick was a relative term, of course. It was well over an hour before her doctor had the chance to come and talk to her again. By then, Flick had been given a sandwich and a cup of tea.

'I'm feeling absolutely fine now,' she told the doctor. 'It *was* just because I skipped breakfast. I won't do that again.'

'Have you noticed any other symptoms in the last couple of weeks? Nausea? Sore breasts? Can you remember when the first day of your last period was?'

The last time Flick could remember even thinking about her period had been when she'd taken her toiletries from her suitcase to put with what she was packing to bring to the Cotswolds and the trickle of fear that ran down her spine arrived at the same moment she realised that her last period had been while she'd still been in Australia.

That tiny alarm bell was there again but this time it was ringing loudly enough to drown out everything else. Flick could feel herself going pale—the way she had only last night, when she'd knelt beside Lachlan, not knowing whether he was still breathing or not. That same reaction was an echo in her head as well, even as she could feel a welcome numbness sweeping in to protect her from trying to cope all at once with something that could have catastrophic repercussions in her life. Something she'd never thought she'd have to think about again.

No...

She didn't need this doctor to confirm the news she was warning her was coming but it was probably something that had to be done.

'I'm sorry if it's a shock for you,' the doctor said gently. 'But there's no mistake. You're definitely pregnant.'

CHAPTER TWELVE

'YOU DON'T HAVE to be here.' Lachlan avoided making any direct eye contact with Josh, who'd been sitting quietly beside his bed for some time now. 'I know I'm not exactly good company.'

It had been a hell of a day with so much happening as his specialists launched him into remission induction with the intention of killing all the AML cells in his blood. He'd started the first day of this frightening twist in his life with a surgical procedure to insert a central venous line just under his collarbone and, this afternoon, Lachlan had spent a couple of hours hooked up to a machine to undergo leukapheresis—a procedure that could rapidly reduce white blood cells counts to provide a head start to chemotherapy designed to achieve remission.

He had never felt this exhausted in his life. The intense medical procedures he'd undergone had been confronting on more than a physical level because he was being forced to face up to the reality of his situation and... it was terrifying.

As a form of escape that he hadn't been able to resist today, Lachlan's thoughts had drifted frequently to catching something far more pleasant to focus on. Like his beloved woodland, with its current carpet of bluebells, or the kitchen of his childhood with its warmth and the lingering aromas of comfort food. The problem with that, however, was that he couldn't think of anything pleasant that didn't include Flick and he was missing her so badly today, it was another level of pain all on its own.

He wanted her to be sitting where Josh was. He wanted her to know that he hadn't meant to hurt her when he'd sent her away. When he'd hurt her by telling her that he didn't need her. Had he really been so dismissive that he'd told her she'd only been employed to care for his mother? But he couldn't give in to the desire to see her again. Not when protecting her from this was perhaps the only way he could show how much he cared about her, even if she would never know.

He cared about Josh, too. More than it should be possible to care about someone he'd only met a matter of weeks ago. But then, he'd had that feeling that half of his life had been stolen—more than that—that he'd been missing half of himself. No wonder it felt so right to have Josh here. And so wrong, for the same reasons it would be wrong to ask Flick to go through this by his side. He knew, without anything being said, that Josh felt the same way about being reunited with his twin. He shouldn't have to go through this, either.

But Josh had other ideas.

'I want to be here.' His tone was a warning not to argue but Lachlan also had other ideas.

'You managed without me in your life for thirty-six years, Josh. It won't be that hard to get used to it again.'

'I don't want to get used to it. You're my brother. The only family I've got.'

'You might have to get used to it.' Lachlan tried a wry laugh but it came out embarrassingly close to a kind of strangled sob. 'Take a leaf out of Flick's book. She's managed to walk away, no problem.'

'Has she? Has she actually gone?'

'Well…she's still here—in the district, at least. Only until we can find another locum nurse. My housekeeper, Mrs Tillman, is sorting that mess out for me.'

Tilly had come to see him late this afternoon. Just a very brief visit, for no more than a minute or two, because she could see how tired Lachlan was and he could see how upset she was.

'You're not going to believe this,' he told Josh, 'but she says Josephine is upset about me. Crocodile tears, huh?'

'I doubt that. Sometimes it takes a shock for people to wake up and see what really matters.'

'Well… I've had a shock and…guess what? Nothing really matters.' Because it was never real, was it? He'd come as close as he ever had in the last few weeks to believing that he could trust the most important things in life, like family—and love—only to find he was about to lose them. Right now, that seemed worse than never having found them at all.

He'd managed alone for his whole life and he could manage this alone too. Especially because anyone else who was too close would only suffer along with him. He knew that Josh was finding the discovery of family connection and the love it represented as significant as he was so he had to persuade his brother to back off and protect himself, even if he had to be cruel to be kind—like he had with Flick.

'Go away, Josh.' This time, Lachlan did make eye contact with his brother. 'Get on with your own life. Get over yourself and marry that nice girl with that astonishing hair.' He managed to find a smile although he couldn't hang on to it because he didn't want Josh to see his lips tremble. 'Go. Be happy for both of us…'

Lachlan desperately needed to sleep. Not simply because exhaustion demanded it but because it was the best way to escape, at least for a little while. But sleep wouldn't come, even long after Josh had gone.

He found himself going over and over their conversation. Had he been right, in suggesting that his mother had been shocked into realising that she did actually care about the adopted son she'd never thought she wanted? Had she pushed him away in the same way as he was pushing both Josh and Flick away from himself now, because he was afraid of the pain that could be experienced on both sides by leaning into having people caring about him? About how much worse it would be to know he had no future when he had people *he* cared deeply about?

He could almost begin to understand.

Begin to forgive…

But still the peace that sleep could bring eluded him. His thoughts drifted from his mother to Josh. From Josh to Flick. Disjointed thoughts, flashes of emotion and— despite everything—a persistent longing, *hope* even, that refused to be dismissed. They were impressions and images, memories and feelings that all felt like pieces of a puzzle that had been tipped, haphazardly, all over a tabletop and were lying, completely jumbled up, in front of him.

Lachlan had no idea where to start to try and put them together but, in the moments as sleep finally stilled those thoughts, he had the feeling that the picture that puzzle would make might be just out of sight but it was imperative that he find out what it was.

Because it could be the most important thing he would ever see in his life and there was pressure building because he could be running out of time…

It was funny that you could be so numb you couldn't feel anything at all but you could still function well enough that nobody else could tell that your life had fallen apart. But, then, the people around her had enough on their minds already, didn't they?

Mrs Tillman overheard the tail end of a conversation with Julia at London Locums the next day when Flick said it might be necessary to line up some candidates to take over Lady Josephine's medical care, but if she disapproved of Flick abandoning the family in a time of crisis she didn't let it show.

'I've got some lovely cheese scones just out of the oven,' was all she said. 'Make sure you have one, won't you, with a cup of tea?'

'I'm really not hungry, thank you.'

'I'm not sure if Lady J. wants to come down for her dinner tonight but it's in the oven for later. I'm off up to Cheltenham to see how our Lachlan's getting on. When we rang earlier, they said he was starting treatment already, poor lad. But that's a good thing, isn't it? Starting treatment early?'

Flick nodded. 'The sooner the better.'

Lady Josephine hadn't wanted to go downstairs for dinner.

'Unless you're eating something, Felicity?'

'I'm not really hungry.'

'Neither am I. But I can't really miss a meal, can I? Not if I'm taking proper care of myself.'

'You're doing very well,' Flick told her. 'Even with all this new upset, you haven't had an asthma attack or any chest pain and your blood glucose levels are a lot more stable than I would have expected.'

'I want to be able to take care of myself.' Lady Josephine took in a quick breath. 'I want to be able to take care of Lachlan, if he'll let me. I didn't do a very good job of that when he was a child, did I? Maybe I can make up for it, at least a little.' She wasn't looking at Flick as she spoke, she was staring out of her window at that view across the gardens towards the woods. 'I'm feeling older today,' she added softly. So softly Flick barely heard. 'And I'm lonely...'

She pretended not to have heard, in case commenting on the admission embarrassed Lady Josephine. 'I'll bring your dinner up on a tray,' she said. 'Maybe some for both of us. And, after that, maybe we could have a game of Scrabble?'

Lady Josephine caught her gaze then and her voice was much stronger. 'I knew you were brave the first time I met you. Feisty. I liked that about you right from the start.' Her smile softened her face so that she looked like a very different woman from the one Flick had first met. 'You've changed something in this house,' she added. 'You've brought life back into it. Even some music and dancing and I don't want to lose that again. I want Lachlan to forgive me one day. Do you think that might be even possible?'

'He loves you,' Flick told her. 'That's why it hurt so much to be told he hadn't been wanted. But, I also think, if you love someone enough, then anything's possible.'

It was probably the thing that Lady Josephine had said that she might not have intended to have been overheard that punctured the safe, numb cocoon Flick had wrapped around her heart.

I'm lonely...

The words came back in the middle of another sleepless night to echo in the silence of her room. More than echo—they resonated deep within Flick because she was lonely too. She had been ever since she'd lost Patrick but she'd never stayed still long enough to let herself think about it. She'd run away from the realisation just as effectively as she'd run from getting involved with someone. And, okay, she'd talked to Julia today about moving on from this position in the McKendry household but she couldn't run this time, could she?

Her hand moved to lie gently on top of her belly.

How could she run when she'd be taking something so precious away from someone she cared about so much?

There was nothing more precious than a baby.

A new life.

Something to live for.

Tears were streaming down Flick's cheeks now. If nothing else, Lachlan had the right to know that he was going to be a father. That, even if he didn't win this battle, there was a part of him who would still be in the world. Being cherished.

But, oh…the pain that was seeping in as the numbness lifted was unbearable. She'd have to pull herself together before she went to see Lachlan. He had more than enough to deal with without her making things worse.

Without knowing she was doing it, Mrs Tillman backed her up.

'The world hasn't ended, lovey,' she told Flick the next morning as she put a cup of coffee in front of her. 'Goodness me, I think Lachlan looked happier when I went to visit him than you do at the moment.'

'How was he feeling?'

'He said nothing hurt, he was just very, very tired. He'd had some extraordinary thing done to him where they take out all your blood and spin it around so fast all the cells separate and they take out the bad ones and then put all the blood back. I really didn't understand how they could do that. He's going to start on the chemotherapy next and I expect that will be harder. Are you going to visit him?'

Flick nodded. 'I'll ring and see if he's allowed visitors.'

Apparently, the only visiting hours allowed were mid-afternoon and early evening. Flick picked up her car keys to head

into town in the afternoon but ended up sitting in her car, having not even turned on
the engine, as she tried, and failed, to decide
how she was going to tell Lachlan what he
needed to know and how he might react.
When she tried, she failed not to let herself
be totally overcome by fear. And grief. Old,
remembered grief but worse—this new one
that was so sharp it was threatening to shred
her heart into ribbons.

She sat in her car for so long she could see
that the sun was sinking below the canopy
of the tallest trees in the woodlands as she
walked from the garage back to the entrance
to the house. Without thinking, she changed
direction, her shoes crunching on the pebbled paths and then silent on the grass lawns
as she made her way into the woods, retrac-
ing the path that Lachlan had taken her on
when he'd introduced her to the magic of
the bluebells.

The flowers were past their best now,
weeks later, but there were still enough to
be a soft haze of blue covering the ground
between the dark trunks of the trees, lit up

by shafts of sunshine that pushed their way through small branches and clouds of leaves. Flick found the exact spot that Lachlan had taken her to and she had to close her eyes and stand very still as the scent surrounded her and memories crowded in with the deep breath she took.

Like that first time in many years that she'd encountered this scent, when she'd buried her nose in those flowers in the jam jar that Lachlan had picked as a gift for her after they'd made love for the first time.

The night their baby had most likely been conceived…

The time Flick had realised that things were changing. That her body was coming back to life and, with the benefit of hindsight, that it *was* possible that she could risk her heart and fall in love again.

Opening her eyes, she could almost see Lachlan here with her as she remembered telling him about the baby she'd lost and how losing the man she loved as well had broken her too much to ever be able to put those pieces back together again. But then he'd held her and, while she might not have recognised it at the time, that had been when the distance between those broken pieces had begun to shrink.

Flick was barely aware of the tears still rolling slowly down her face as she stooped and picked a flower and then another. By the time she had three blooms between her fingers, she was remembering seeing a tiny bouquet like this on Lady Josephine's table and that had been the moment she'd realised that those pieces had been put back together. That she was totally in love with Lachlan and that she couldn't run away. She could hear an echo of Lady Josephine's words, too, about those flowers.

'They smelt like tears...'

But to Flick they still smelt like a new beginning. Still holding those few blooms, she wrapped her arms around herself as she took another deep breath, soaking in the scent.

And that reminded her of that night in the ballroom and the way Lachlan had been looking at her after that magical, barefoot dance together with Lachlan's shirt unbuttoned and her wearing that gloriously swirly blue dress.

You could only look at someone you loved like that.

He did love her, didn't he? Had he pushed her away because he was trying to protect her from the possibility of having to relive the devastation of losing Patrick? The experience she'd told him had been so unbearable she had learned to run from getting that close to anyone ever again?

But surely that was her choice to make?

What if the shoe had been on the other foot and she was the one who'd been given a scary diagnosis? How much worse would it be to face something like that without someone who cared by your side? She remembered how helpless it had made her feel not being able to change the outcome with Patrick but why hadn't she thought about the gift she'd given by being there with him for every possible moment and loving him until the very end?

Would she want Lachlan to be with her—to hold her in his arms—even if she knew he'd been through heartbreak like that before? Of course she would—but only if he wanted to be there and if he felt strong enough to stay, and that would have to be entirely his own choice. She would never have put pressure on him by asking.

That was what Lachlan was doing, she realised. He had given her a way out. A chance to run. The space to make that choice for herself. Flick brushed away the last tears on her face and could feel her strength gathering. Perhaps she'd already made that choice when she'd come here to a place that was always going to be filled with memories of this new love in her life. Or perhaps that should be simply a new life…

Along with the strength came a new resolution. Lachlan couldn't be allowed to assume that the worst was going to happen, either. Life was full of unexpected twists and turns. For heaven's sake, he'd discovered that he had an identical twin brother and it was already obvious that they had formed a strong bond. There was also a very real possibility that Josh could be a perfect match for a stem cell transplant and a complete cure for Lachlan. And it could be that she and Lachlan had a future ahead of them that they could dream about like any other couple in love.

If she was right, that was, and he was in love with her.

She had to find that out for sure, mind you, but she knew she'd know the moment she walked into that hospital room and caught his gaze because there were so many things they could say to each other without actually speaking any words. Flick found herself smiling as she crouched down again to pick a few more flowers to add to the ones in her hand. Maybe it was a bit of a cliché to take a bouquet as a gift when you went to visit someone in hospital but this was different.

It was personal.

Some couples had a special song that was deeply significant to them both. She and Lachlan McKendry had a flower...

Sometimes, success was not something that you could celebrate at all.

Who knew?

Lachlan lay in his bed, alone in his private hospital room, feeling more alone than he had ever felt in his entire life. It had been another long day and he'd had doctors and nurses and technicians around him as they planned and then started a chemotherapy regime that would hopefully put him into remission in the shortest possible time, but now he was alone.

Because he'd been so successful in pushing the people that really mattered out of his life.

Visiting hours this afternoon had come and gone with nobody arriving. Evening hours had started a while back now and, again, there was nobody. He'd tried calling Josh a little while ago, with the intention of apologising for what he'd said last night, but his brother hadn't picked up. He hadn't even had a text message from Josh, which he couldn't really be surprised by since he'd told him to go away and get on with his own life. He didn't have any right to expect that Flick would front up, either, when he'd basically told her that she wasn't needed. Or wanted.

And these were good things, Lachlan tried to reassure himself. It was what he'd wanted, wasn't it? That he could handle this on his own. That he wouldn't drag anyone else along on what could potentially be a rough journey. The only downside of being left with nothing but his own thoughts to distract him was…well…he was thinking too much.

About what life had been like only a matter of weeks ago. About how his professional life had been exactly what he'd always dreamed of it being and the only major worries in his personal life had been that his mother had kept antagonising and then dismissing her carers and that his current female companion had made the fatal mistake of wanting to talk about their 'future'. Good grief…he had to think for a moment before he could remember her name. Sharon? Cheryl? No… Shayna.

Lachlan sent a silent apology out into the universe but then he found his mouth twisting into a wry kind of smile. What wouldn't he give to be able to talk about a 'future' with someone now? Or 'family', which was another one of the 'F' words he'd believed he never wanted to apply to his own personal life. He could still count the hours since that final, dramatic twist in his life and the shock had stripped everything irrelevant away, leaving him with a perspective on life that was stunningly simple in its clarity.

The work that he loved so much mattered, of course. He could change lives and do amazing things for others but…what really mattered when you were faced with something *this* huge was who actually cared about *you* and not just about what you had done with your life.

How many times had he heard or read about people losing their battle with a terminal illness where there was comfort to be found in the simple sentence that they'd been surrounded by their friends and family.

More 'F' words. And what was even more ironic was that there was another one that simply wouldn't be silenced. One that he could feel, even more than he could hear echoing in the back of his head, especially when he was alone like this and when he closed his eyes.

Flick... Felicity... *Flick*...

Maybe he'd whispered her name out loud without realising it but the last thing he'd expected to hear was her voice, unless that was also in his imagination?

'I'm here, Lachlan.'

His eyes flew open but, because he was lying down, the first thing he saw was a bunch of slightly bedraggled bluebells. They looked as if they were almost ready to drop their petals. As if their stalks had been clutched a little too tightly for a little too long. They were also the most beautiful things Lachlan had ever seen. Because he couldn't see them without remembering the way he'd held Flick in his arms that day in the woods. About the way she'd climbed into his heart and pulled the door closed behind her so that there was no way she would ever leave it.

No… Maybe that had been when the door had been pulled tightly shut but she had reached a space in his heart and soul well before that. When she'd seen him for exactly who he was—a man who'd been so damaged by never feeling loved—and she had taken him into *her* arms and he'd known that he could never truly give up on wanting to be loved.

He'd believed that he never wanted a family.

But the truth was the complete opposite. It had been the only thing he'd ever truly wanted.

Lachlan raised his eyes to meet Flick's and realised they were almost the same colour as the flowers she held in her hands. They were also shining very brightly with unshed tears.

'I had to come,' she said softly. 'And I'm not leaving you again. I love you too much to do that.'

'Oh…thank God,' Lachlan breathed. He couldn't look away from those eyes. He wanted to soak in the love he could see there until it filled every cell in his body. 'I only told you to go because it was the only way I could think to show you how much I love *you.*'

'I can think of a much better way.' The tears were escaping from Flick's eyes but she was smiling.

Those bluebells somehow got scattered over the covers as Flick found space to squeeze in beside Lachlan on his bed so that they could just lie there and hold each other, their heads so close together on his pillows that their foreheads were touching.

'You're right.' Lachlan felt too weak to do anything other than accept Flick's gentle kiss but he could keep his arms around her and feel the way she was holding him. 'This is a much better way.'

'That's not what I meant.' He could feel Flick's breasts push against his arm as she took a deep breath. 'I've got something to tell you.'

'You just told me the most important thing you could ever say.' Not that Lachlan would ever tire of hearing her tell him how much she loved him. In fact, he needed to hear it again. 'But don't stop,' he added. 'Don't ever stop. I promise I won't, either. I love you, Flick. I love you *so* much.'

'I'm pregnant,' Flick whispered. 'You're going to be a father, Lachlan.'

Oh...*man*... He hadn't seen that coming. An 'F' word that hadn't even entered his head. One that eclipsed all others but included them, as well. Father. Family. *Future*...

A future that was more than worth fighting for.

'That's what I meant.' Flick's voice wobbled. 'We're going to win this battle. Because I need you. Our baby needs you.'

This was breaking her heart—in a good way.

That they wouldn't win the battle ahead of them was not going to be allowed any head space right now but what was making her heart full enough to burst was the realisation that *these* were exactly the kind of moments that mattered. That made life so worth living.

Flick hadn't been embracing moments like this in too long but she wasn't going to miss any more of them. She was going to make the most of every single one. Lachlan was still in a stunned silence. Or maybe he just needed to rest? Flick touched his face with a gentle stroke of her fingers.

'So, there I was, in the bluebells,' she said, so softly that only the man she loved could hear her words. 'And I'm thinking about you meeting our baby. Seeing his—or her—first smile and taking their first step. About taking them to school on their first day. Being part of a family. The way you and Josh should have been, with parents who loved you so much you'd always know how wanted you were.'

Flick could feel Lachlan's arm tighten around her. She could feel, rather than see, the tear that escaped his eye because she still had her forehead resting against his and her nose touching his. She was too close to see what the expression was in his eyes, but that didn't matter because she could feel exactly how he felt. She could feel them exchanging strength. Making silent vows to do whatever it took to make sure they were both there to welcome that new life and nurture it with the kind of love they had found in each other.

'We'll celebrate everything,' she added. 'Birthdays and weddings. Christmas and… and…'

'Bluebells?'

'Yes…' A huff of laughter escaped Flick. 'We'll celebrate bluebell season. Every year.' She had her own tears escaping again now and she knew they were mingling with Lachlan's. 'I said something to your mother yesterday when she asked me if I thought it might be possible that you could forgive her one day.'

She paused for a heartbeat, worried that Lachlan might pull away at the reminder of past hurts, but, to her surprise, she felt his muscles soften a little.

'What was that?'

'That if you love someone enough, then anything's possible.'

'You make anything possible, Felicity Stephens,' Lachlan said quietly. 'You make life something that I never even imagined it could be. Not for me, anyway.'

Flick had to swallow hard. If only she could do the one thing Lachlan needed more than anything at this point in his life—give him the one thing that could mean he would be around to celebrate all the things that she was dreaming of sharing with him.

She probably couldn't, although she would get herself tested as a potential donor for a stem cell transplant, of course.

But maybe she wouldn't even need to do that.

They both heard the gentle tap on the door of Lachlan's hospital room. Flick didn't get off the bed, so she was still in Lachlan's arms as his twin brother came into the room. He wasn't alone. He was holding Stevie's hand as they came in and she had her arm around the shoulders of a young boy.

Josh's eyes widened as he took in that Lachlan and Flick were so closely entwined.

'We're interrupting something, aren't we? Maybe we should come back some other time?'

'No…it's okay.' Flick moved, sitting up and sliding her legs off the bed so she ended up just being perched on the side. As she pushed tousled hair off her face, she caught Stevie's gaze. The shared look was that of two women who were totally in love with the men they were with. A look of understanding. And joy. And...hope?

'Sorry I couldn't take your call before,' Josh was saying to Lachlan. 'We had a bit going on there for a while when Mattie here went AWOL.'

'Hi, Mattie.' Lachlan smiled at the serious-looking boy. 'I'm guessing that Stevie's your mum, yes?'

Mattie nodded. And then a smile broke out and lit up his face. 'And Josh's going to be my dad. And...and that means you're going to be my *uncle*.' He made an obvious effort to contain his excitement. 'I'm sorry that you're sick...'

Lachlan and Josh were looking at each other now and Flick could sense a similar kind of silent communication happening that she'd just shared with Stevie. Tears prickled at the back of her eyes as she realised that both these men, with a shared distrust of families and associated happiness, had found someone they could love—who loved *them*—enough to change their lives. Something else they would have in common from now on? A bond that was creating another little miracle by giving them both an extended family. She touched her belly as she smiled at Mattie. This family was already growing...

'That is what we came here to tell you.' Josh put his hand on Mattie's shoulder as he smiled down at him. 'But it's not the only thing.'

'Josh's going to get himself tested.' Mattie looked as though he was bursting with pride. 'He's going to have a hole put into his *bones*.'

'Just one bone,' Stevie put in. She was looking just as proud of Josh as Mattie was. 'To see if he's a match.'

'He will be.' Mattie was beaming now. 'Josh says that nobody could be a better match than an identical twin and it's really lucky that he met you in time because it'll mean that you can hang around and be my uncle for ever.'

That made all the adults in the room laugh.

Josh and Stevie were gazing at each other over Mattie's head. Flick turned to find Lachlan gazing at her and the laughter faded into something that wrapped itself around her heart so tightly she knew it was going to be there as long as she had breath in her body.

Lachlan was going to do everything he could to hang around for ever.

So he could be an uncle to Mattie.

And a brother to Josh.

Maybe even a son to Josephine McKendry.

But, most of all, he was going to be the man who loved *her*. The father of her baby. Her husband…?

'Hey…' Flick was still holding Lachlan's gaze. 'Did we forget something?'

'Yeah… I reckon.'

They were both smiling again as they spoke at exactly the same time. 'Will you marry me?'

They were both laughing as they spoke again, in unison.

'Yes…'

EPILOGUE

Nearly two years later...

THE BLUEBELL SEASON was at the peak of its glory in the woodlands of the McKendry family's Cotswold estate.

There were no small, lonely boys there, gathering a bouquet of the flowers to give to their mother.

There were no sad people there, either, quietly holding each other to share comfort or strength.

Instead, this patch of woodland, which was bathed in the amazing colour and scent of these iconic flowers, had a small and very select group of people, treading carefully when they moved to avoid squashing a single bloom as photographs were being taken to commemorate a wedding service that had just taken place in this magical setting.

There were also two dogs who weren't being nearly as careful with the flowers.

'Come here, Cocoa,' Lady Josephine ordered. 'Just because the ceremony's over, it doesn't mean you can wreck all Jack's hard work.'

Tilly might have been delightedly working for many weeks on the wedding feast awaiting everybody back at the house but her husband had also been busy and he'd constructed a wonderfully rustic arch from fallen branches he'd been collecting in the woods and had then decorated it with ivy and tiny, white roses from the gardens he'd nurtured for decades.

Flick had some of those roses in her wedding bouquet, as well. Along with a cloud of gypsophila and highlighted, of course, with what were now her favourite flowers on earth—the humble bluebell. The tiny lace flowers attached all over the silk chiffon skirt of her wedding dress matched the pattern of the lace bodice but there was nothing to detract from its simplicity. The dress had only spaghetti straps. Her shoes were white ballet slippers and she wore no veil—just a wreath of tiny, white flowers that nestled into her loose, tumble of shoulder length golden waves.

'I'd like one with all the boys this time.' The photographer was grinning. 'If you think you can cope with that, Lachlan?'

'Are you kidding? I've got toddling twins. I'm learning to cope with anything.' He ran to scoop up one of the boys, Liam, who was running after Cocoa, and then turned to try and see where his twin, Ben, had got to.

'I've got him,' Josh called.

'And I've got Lucky.' Mattie had his beloved, scruffy white dog in his arms. 'He's a boy too, isn't he?'

'Sure is.' Josh was trying to brush dirt off Ben's hands. 'Where do you want us?' he asked the photographer.

'Under the arch? No…that old log over there is much better. You sit in the middle, Mattie, and see if Lucky will sit at your feet. We'll have Dad on one side, Uncle on the other and they can each hold a twin.'

It took a while to set the photograph up

to his satisfaction but Flick was more than happy to stand and watch all the boys in her life as they laughed and tried to get close enough to make the photo work.

Stevie came to stand beside her and she was clearly loving this as much as Flick.

'How gorgeous is that?' Her smile was misty.

'We're outnumbered.' Flick shifted her gaze to the impressive roundness of Stevie's belly. 'Thank goodness you're having a girl.'

'If you'd waited a bit longer, she could have been a flower girl for you. How cute would that have been?'

'It feels like we waited too long already. It's been nearly two years.'

'I know. And I know Josh and I rushed off to the registry office in no time flat but that was for Mattie's benefit as much as anything. He needed to trust that us becoming a family was really going to happen. And it had to be just us because…well, you know…'

Flick nodded. 'Seems like for ever ago, thank goodness, but it was a rough few months, wasn't it? Especially getting to that hundred days after the stem cell transplant without any setbacks like infection.'

'Things were just getting manageable and then you went and had twins.'

Flick laughed. 'Who would have guessed that we had another surprise waiting in the wings? At least that was a happy one. And maybe that's why it hit me so suddenly and I fainted that day in the hospital.'

Her smile faded into something far more poignant as she let her gaze settle on her husband. 'Or maybe that was just the shock of thinking I could lose the love of my life…'

As if he felt her gaze on him, Lachlan looked up from where he was trying to prise Liam's fingers off one of his shirt buttons. The smile the two of them shared seemed to be the reason that Stevie had to brush a tear from beneath her eye.

'Josh always said that he was going to get a perfect result from being lucky enough to have a twin brother as a donor and look at him now—I reckon he *can* cope with anything at all. He's looking so well. And *so* happy…'

A peal of baby laughter came from the group on the log as Lucky leaned out of Mattie's arms to lick Liam's face.

'That's going to make a gorgeous photo.' Lady Josephine had come to stand beside Flick and Stevie. 'Just as well I put Cocoa back on her lead, though. She would have knocked them both over.'

The six-month-old chocolate Labrador had proved a valuable addition to the therapy that Lachlan's mother had been more than prepared to embrace as her contribution to the building of a new family. Now, nearly two years later, she was barely recognisable as the lonely, older woman who'd struggled with mental health issues for far too long. She was a beloved grandmother, not only to the twins but to Mattie as well. And Stevie was as much a part of this family as Lachlan's twin brother.

'It's a shame your mother wasn't up to travelling yet after her hip surgery, Stevie. But Josh tells me you've almost got the cottage ready for her to move into.'

'Just a few final touches to make.' Stevie nodded. 'It all took far longer than we expected. The council can make you wait a long time for permission to do things to listed houses but it's all worked out perfectly in the end. Mum will have moved in by the time this one arrives—' she patted her belly '—and it was even better than the Big Brother programme for building a bond between Josh and Mattie as they tackled all their projects. I gave them matching leather tool belts that first Christmas we had together and they were both over the moon.'

The photographer had finished that shot. 'Let's have one more of the bride and groom,' he called. 'How 'bout you sit amongst the bluebells—or will that ruin your dress?'

Lachlan carried Liam towards his mother. 'Can you take him for a minute, Grandma?'

'Might be safer if someone else did.'

Lachlan's eyebrows rose. 'You're not feeling unwell, are you? Did you check your BGL this morning?'

'Of course I did. You know perfectly well my diabetes is under excellent control. I just happen to be holding a rather large and not particularly well-behaved young dog.'

'I'll take him.' Mattie had grown several inches in the last two years. 'I'm going to be a big brother soon, so I could kind of use the practice.'

Lachlan handed the toddler over. 'You'll be a fabulous big brother. Just like your dad.'

'How do you know I was born first?' Josh was grinning as he joined them.

'I was talking about how you met Mattie in the first place. Don't think you were born first, mate, but I guess that's something we'll never know.'

'Just as well. We need something to argue about.' Josh smiled down at Mattie as Lachlan took Flick's hand to lead her back to the photographer. 'How 'bout we take these wee fellows into the house? It's getting a bit colder.'

'That's where I'm heading.' Mrs Tillman was walking past. 'I need to see what's going on in my kitchen.'

'Let's all go.' Stevie smiled. 'I reckon our

bride and groom might appreciate a quiet moment on their own when their photos are finally done.'

But they were actually getting a quiet moment already, as the photographer set up a longer distance shot and everybody else set off on the woodland track that would lead them back to the house.

Flick was watching them leave. Her mother-in-law, who she had such a special bond with, given how much they understood of each other's past lives. Her brother-in-law whom she loved anyway for being so like Lachlan and she could never thank him enough for making Lachlan's complete cure a possibility. She had to thank him for marrying Stevie, too, because the two women had become far more than sisters-in-law. They were best friends. And family. There were her two beloved sons as well, peering back over their uncle and cousin's shoulders, watching as they were taken temporarily out of sight of their parents.

And then Flick looked up at the person

who was closest to her. Not just physically but a part of her heart and soul. The man she loved so much she'd had tears of joy on her face as they'd exchanged their vows, using their own twist on vows that hadn't lost their beauty by becoming so well known.

'You will feel no rain, because I will be your shelter...'

'You will feel no cold, because I will be your warmth...'

'You will never be lonely, because even when we're not together I will be with you, in your heart...'

'We are two people but we have one life before us.'

'I love you...'

She had tears shining in her eyes as she held Lachlan's gaze now.

'Do you remember the first time you brought me here to see the bluebells? Because you said they smelt even better in the woods?'

'How could I ever forget?' Lachlan's smile was as tender as the kiss he bent to place on Flick's lips. 'I was already in love with you—I just didn't realise it.'

'Do you remember what I said?'

'Tell me again.'

'That we all have our stories and real life isn't a fairy tale so they don't always have happy endings.'

'I remember.'

'But it's not true, is it? Not for us, anyway.' Flick's smile wobbled. 'The day I arrived here and we had some of Tilly's wonderful food in the kitchen and I was half-asleep from jet lag, I really did think I'd stepped into some kind of fairy tale. And maybe it's been hard and it's not an ending but just a beginning but… I've never felt this happy in my life.'

'Neither have I.'

Lachlan kissed her again and it was so quiet in the woods they could hear the camera clicks of this moment being recorded for ever from the other side of the clearing. But they both felt as if they were totally alone together as they ended that kiss and smiled mistily at each other.

'Am I the prince?' Lachlan asked.

'I guess you have to be.' Flick nodded.

'That makes you my princess, doesn't it? Mind you, I already knew that, because… you know…you're wearing that gorgeous dress.'

'I am.'

'Are you going to be able to dance in that dress? Mother's expecting us to show off that perfect waltz we've been practising.'

'I know. I'd better hope I don't get nervous and stand on your toes like I did the first time.'

'I don't care if you do.' Lachlan swept Flick up into his arms, turning towards the photographer so that he could capture what had to look like pure joy, because that was exactly what it was. 'I love you, Mrs McKendry.'

'I love you, too, Mr McKendry.'

'Do you think it's time we went and found the rest of our family?'

'I do.'

'Maybe I'd better carry you. Just so you don't stand on my toes.'

Flick snuggled into his arms so that her head fitted into that delicious hollow just over his heart where she could feel it beating against her cheek.

'I think that's a very good idea...'

* * * * *

LET'S TALK
Romance

For exclusive extracts, competitions and special offers, find us online:

f facebook.com/millsandboon

⧉ @millsandboonuk

🐦 @millsandboon

Or get in touch on 0844 844 1351*

For all the latest titles coming soon, visit millsandboon.co.uk/nextmonth